DENTAL TOURISM

Dental Tourism

MARK O'FLYNN

PUNCHER & WATTMANN

First published in 2020

Published by Puncher and Wattmann
PO Box 279
Waratah NSW 2298
http://www.puncherandwattmann.com
puncherandwattmann@bigpond.com

ISBN 978-1-925780-53-6

 A catalogue record for this book is available from the National Library Australia.

Cover design by Miranda Douglas
Typeset by Christine Bruderlin
Text set in Minion Pro
Printed by Lightning Source International

This project has been assisted by the Australian Government through the Australia Council, its arts funding and advisory body.

Contents

Though there are torturers
in the world
there are also musicians.

—Michael Coady, *Though There are Torturers*
(from *Oven Lane*)

For Barb

PART ONE

The Eagle

We're in the car driving out through the western district towards the Grampians where Stuart used to love to come. For someone raised in the suburbs it's hard to credit how Stuart formed such an affection for the Grampians. For the country. Stuart liked birds. John Gould Club and all that. And we've sure seen plenty of those scattered along the sides of the road, dead feathers wafting in the breeze. Hugh, my brother, is driving. He won't let me behind the wheel because it's a company car and the insurance wouldn't cover him letting anyone else drive. Hugh likes to control things. He is in real estate and so does a lot of driving, although I don't know how much of that he does in the country. He doesn't like dirt roads. I don't think Stuart has been in a company car before. I don't mind. I don't want to drive. I'm too raw, split open like a bag of rice. Hugh is driving and I am the passenger and Stuart is in a box on my lap. I would not let

Hugh put him in the boot. He's quite heavy. At least the remains of him are. His ashes. I've come to think of this burden as almost comforting. To nurse him. It is the last thing I am able to do for him. Our brother. Well, second last. Scattering the ashes will be the last thing.

Stuart used to come to the Grampians to bushwalk and watch birds. He may well have brought women up here, but it would have been a brave sort of girl to come all this way to watch birds, and none have been forthcoming about that. Mt. Arapiles, he told us to general tedium, is a great sanctuary for all sorts of raptors and members of the parrot family, Rosellas, Lorikeets and so on. His final wish, against that of our elderly parents, was to have his ashes scattered off Signal Rock, which rises up like an ice cream cone dropped on the ground, or the weird eye of a chameleon. Our father wants the ashes to remain in the family home, on the mantelpiece where Mum can be reminded of them—of *him*, of *him*. An idea for which Hugh has a great deal of sympathy. However, this is Stuart's wish, so instead we take out a spoonful, blue-grey they are, and put them in a little bottle that Mum can keep in her pocket and beside her bed. The remainder of his possessions Stuart didn't care what we did with.

Once, when we were eight, ten and thirteen years old, with me the youngest and Hugh the eldest, we were playing cricket in the front driveway. Rather than risk whacking the ball onto the road, we bowl from the southern end, namely the house. The house serves as a useful midfielder. It's out if you belt it over the roof, or onto the roof. And there'll be repercussions if you hit it into the fuchsias. Stuart is whacking them regularly into Mum's windows.

It is only a tennis ball so they don't break, just make a loud, glassy thump as if they'd like to. The noise inside must sound ominous.

Eventually Mum comes out and says, 'Is that you hitting the ball into the windows Stuart? Or is it a bird?'

After a while Stuart replies, 'A bird.'

'What sort of a bird?' asks Mum. 'I hope it's not that little blue wren. It'll break its neck if it's not careful.'

'No,' says Stuart, and I have to say I respect him for this. 'It was an eagle. A wedge-tailed eagle.'

And Mum almost falls for it.

The trees and fences slide by. I can imagine the updraughts and thermals swirling high above the yellow paddocks of the western plains. Hugh wants to turn on the radio, but I'd rather not. His comfort zone is left behind at the bitumen.

I respected Stuart's readiness to pursue the adventure. He was a schoolboy hero for me and a nightmare for our mother. He was a great outdoorsman, unlike Hugh or I who have pursued other interests. Camping by himself for days on end in the most inhospitable places. The rougher the better; the rougher the purer. I suspect he was the sort of ratbag survivalist who ate road kill, or at least endorsed it. Another story he used to tell us before he got sick he didn't care if we believed or not. His capacity for self-conviction was so strong that when the anecdote was retold at the funeral it's like the yarn itself was daring someone to call out *bullshit*.

He's out camping one summer in the forest near Rose Creek. He wants to find a powerful owl. It's way past midnight when the roar of a bushfire approaching wakes him. It has dropped off the escarpment and is travelling fast. Smoke and embers everywhere.

He only has time to put on one shoe before the flames are on him, so he jumps into a water hole in the creek. As he sits there, up to his neck, the flames leaping over him, a kangaroo suddenly splashes into the water beside him. Then a snake, a red-bellied black snake slides in too.

How did he know what sort of snake it was? Hugh wants to know.

The light of the flames allows him to identify the species. It's only a small water hole and the three of them try to keep their distance from each other, especially the snake. After the fire passes, the focus comes back to the occupants of the water hole. They look at each other. Then, almost with a polite nod, the snake slithers out into the glowing darkness. The kangaroo also struggles out of the water, then hops off tentatively through the smoke, while Stuart continues to sit there feeling pretty pleased with himself. He always says he admires the way different creatures can harmonise in the face of adversity, that cooperation is a greater force for survival than aggression and fear. Hugh says he is a left-over hippie and ought to think about investment.

This story, or one like it, is going through my mind as we park the car adjacent to a dry and dusty paddock near the Boronia Trail. We get out to stretch our legs before the ascent. There is a daylight moon in the sky.

'What's that?' Hugh asks.

I follow his pointing finger. A little way beyond the fence something is thrashing on the ground, like a pudding cloth boiling in a copper. I think at first it is two animals fighting, but as we look it becomes apparent that it is one animal fighting with itself. A bird. We go to the fence and the mystery is resolved. It is a wedge-tailed eagle, caught in a trap of some sort.

'Shit,' says Hugh, amazed.

The tan feathers of the breast and wings are ruffled as the great bird rolls in the dust flapping frantically, struggling to take off. However, the trap—it's a rabbit trap—is firmly chained to the ground. We climb through the fence and approach it cautiously. The eagle stands up and watches us. It spreads its wings which are two metres wide at least. Its long legs are firmly caught in the teeth of the trap.

'Jesus,' says Hugh, 'will you look at that?'

'Amazing,' I say.

'What'll we do?'

'We can't just leave it there.'

'Darren, I think actually we can,' says Hugh. 'Don't the farmers hate those things?'

'Bugger the farmers. It'll die if we leave it there. Stuart thought they were majestic.'

'Stuart isn't here.'

I turn and look back at the car.

'Stuart would want us to help it,' I say. I am not above seeing the symbolism of this.

'Are you crazy? You open that trap and it'll tear your face off. Those talons are like razor blades. I know,' he has a light-bulb moment. 'Let's ring the wildlife rescue people.'

Hugh likes taking charge of situations. He flips open his phone, prods a few numbers, listens, prods a few more, holds it to his ear again. The bird watches every move.

'No signal.'

'That's technology for you.'

'Try your phone.'

'I didn't bring it,' I say.

'Why not?'

'I don't want Julie to ring me.'

'Why not? She's your wife, isn't she?'

'It's a long story.'

'Now you tell me.'

'No. I don't want to tell you. It's none of your business. We're here for Stuart.'

'Shit.'

We stare at the bird and the bird stares at us. It is as tall as an angry adolescent. I'm reminded of that Dianne Arbus picture of the incensed boy holding a hand grenade.

Hugh says, 'I think we should belt it with a shovel.'

'Piss off. It's beautiful.'

'Put it out of its misery.'

'It doesn't look too miserable to me,' I say. 'It looks downright cranky.'

'It's the easiest solution.'

'Did you bring a shovel? Do real estate agents drive around with shovels in their cars?'

'Point taken. What about a stick?'

'No.'

'A branch.'

'Hugh, what would Stuart think of you?'

'Well what do you suggest? I wanted to leave him home on

the mantelpiece where Mum could have a good weep over him.'

I do not respond to this. I know he's baiting me in what I recognise is a kind of maddened grief. I have it too.

'Let's leave the trap on. Chuck a blanket over it. Take it back to Hall's Gap. There's bound to be a wildlife rescue place there. Or even a vet. At a pinch we leave it with the cops. Hugh, this is meant to be.'

'We haven't got a blanket.'

'Yes we have. There's one in the back seat.'

'No there isn't.'

'Yes there is.'

'Do you want me to prove it to you?'

'I'd love you to prove it to me.'

'Look, I don't think it's going to sit calmly in the back seat.'

Hugh is running out of options.

'I'll hold it,' I say. 'Stuart would have had it out of there by now. Come on. As long as its feet are secure, they're the dangerous bit.'

'You're crazy.'

Unconvinced, Hugh returns to the car, climbing between the strands of fencing wire.

I look at the eagle and want to talk to it, but I don't know what to say. Only Stuart could have got away with that. Fucking Stuart, look what he's done. Hugh soon comes back with the picnic blanket, tartan, which suddenly looks extremely feeble.

'There you go David Attenborough.'

He also has a big heavy stick. More grief.

'What's that for?'

'Just in case.'

'Great.'

'You all right?'

'No.'

I circle the tethered eagle, but it turns with me, rattling the chain in the dust, eye to eye.

'Try to sneak up on it.'

'I am trying.'

I take my jumper off and hold it like a gladiator holding a mesh net—an *iaculum*—I know that much, but that's merely an occupational hazard. An academic one that probably won't be of much use here.

'What's that for?'

'The feet.'

Hugh waves his arms and the eagle turns and glares, sensing the Judas in him. In that moment I take a step forward and, gently as a magician, waft the blanket over the eagle's head. It immediately stands stock still and I am able to wrap my big bear's arms about it thereby holding its wings to its sides.

'The feet, the feet,' I squawk.

Hugh quickly throws my jumper over the lethal looking talons and the trap. He pulls free the peg anchoring the chain to the ground and wraps it, Houdini style, around the trap, the legs and my jumper in a neat little parcel. Well done, I think. I pick up the bundle and lurch to my feet. Together with the trap it must weigh six kilos or more.

Negotiating the fence is awkward, but luckily it is old and rusty. Hugh is able to stretch apart the two bottom strands, which enables me to combine a sort of rolling action with an infant elbow crawl, and I squeeze through. The bird gives an affronted cough at this undignified treatment. I hope I haven't squashed it, but it seems okay. Hugh holds the car door open and I slide into the back seat. The hooded bird sits up straight and still and one may as well say proud, even though it is under a blanket, at the sound of the door slamming. It seems suddenly much larger here in the confined space of the car. Hugh jumps like a rally driver into the front seat and guns the engine. He has always secretly liked a bit of drama. He turns back down the road and accelerates. He must be worried about the insurance because he yells, 'Don't let it shit.'

I don't bother to answer. I've got, as the saying goes, my hands full. Beneath the blanket the eagle seems agitated at the motion of the car. It wriggles its head and neck back and forth as I pin its wings to its sides. I wish Stuart was here to let us know whether it is male or female, what sort of whistle will calm it down. Then I remember he is.

We come up behind a car which appears ahead and Hugh indicates he is going to overtake.

'Careful Hugh, I haven't got a seat belt on.'

He immediately slows down. At that moment the eagle finds a gap in the tartan blanket and out pops its head. It looks like it is wearing a Scottish poncho. I study the tawny feathers at the neck, fulvous I think they're called. Slowly the eagle turns its head, owl-like, a full hundred and eighty degrees and looks me straight in the eye.

I freeze. Its beak, which is a creamy colour, is huge and pointy, like something an Elizabethan dentist might use, and here I was worried about the talons at the other end. It is barely six inches from my face. It could take my eye, my nose, Jesus it could take out my tongue if it wanted, but it doesn't. It just glares at me. I am acutely aware of one of the eagle's talons slowly squeezing my thigh through the cushion of my jumper.

It revolves its head again and looks at the back of Hugh's skull. It could have his ear in a whisker. Suddenly Hugh slams on the brakes as the car in front makes an unanticipated right hand turn. This causes several things to happen in quick succession.

'Prick!' Hugh shouts.

The eagle's head hits the seat in front of it; my head gives the bird a sound thump on the back of the neck. I can smell the dust in its feathers. And the box containing Stuart's ashes rolls off the front seat on to the passenger side floor. I cannot tell if the ashes have spilled because I am watching the eagle rip great gobbets of vinyl out of the back of Hugh's headrest. The bird suddenly flexes its wings and stretches them out beneath the blanket hitting both windows at the same time. The blanket slides off its shoulders like a magician's cloak and I hold it up now, not to contain the eagle, but to protect myself, perhaps to hide behind.

'That bastard didn't indicate,' curses Hugh. Then, 'What the hell is going on back there?'

'Drive Hugh,' I call, not wanting him to turn around at the moment. 'Just drive.'

The eagle stares at me as if it knows, better than I do myself, exactly what I am thinking.

The Milkman's Son

He grows up in Marrickville. The laneways are safe to walk down even at night. His father is Mr Fitz, the hairy man. He is the milkman. He gets up very early when everyone else is fast asleep. He takes milk from the dairy on his horse and cart and delivers it to all the sleeping families around Marrickville and Dulwich Hill. When the boys are of age, (there are several of them) Mr Fitz takes them with him. To teach them the trade. The true meaning of work and, in a strange way, the grace in it. The value of sacrifice.

One morning, when he is of age, his father creeps into his room. The birds have not woken. His brother asleep in the next bed. There is condensation on the window. Mr Fitz has been up for over an hour, watering the horse, feeding the horse, harnessing the horse. The clink and rattle of its straps and buckles at the bottom of the yard by the lane. It is 1933. The milk must be delivered.

Mr Fitz stands at the foot of their beds. The hair is licked up at the backs of their heads. They nuzzle the pillow with their open mouths. The predawn slack-jawed dream. One boy's eyes twitch. The other mumbles something. Mr Fitz gently untucks the sheets at the foot end of one bed, hmm, which one today? He eases his freezing hands into the warm burrow. He grips Dave's naked feet, who yelps in shock, jerking his knees up to his chest. The icy predators find his feet again and latch on. The other boy, Gerald, wakes in sympathy. It will be his turn tomorrow.

'Wake up now, lads. Wake up, your tea is gone cold.'

'Ged orf,' blurts the boy, clinging to the blankets.

'Rise and shine my lad. Ups a daisy.'

'Ged orf.'

Mr Fitz tickles Dave through the blankets, then whips them back to let the bitter night air gnaw at him. He looks down on his son. An oyster scooped out of its shell, curled up on the bed like a question mark.

Dave dresses quickly. Rearranges the stranglehold the scapular has around his neck. In the kitchen his father hands him a mug of lukewarm tea. Mr Fitz sits down at the table before the open ledger. The boy wraps his hands about the chipped mug. There is a piece of bread and dripping. His mother's presence palpable in the quiet upstairs. Mr Fitz is wearing shorts. His knees callused and blue and numb with the cold.

Dave thinks of his mother asleep in her big bed. The younger children will be allowed to join her when they wake, but for Dave the long day has begun. His father licks his thumb and turns a giant page of the ledger. It is a marvellous looking thing, a book of smells,

14

with the edges of the pages all varicose and marbled like feathers. Inside he knows all the names: Atkins, Poole, Lalor, Flemming, O'Leary, Divola, Killom, all the names down one column. The days of the week and balance due stretching across the top of the page: 46p, 24p, 6p, 41p, 40p, 43p, 38p respectively and so on for all the other people. Big effort to turn the page. Dave sometimes wonders how the Killoms got their name. Possibly, he considers, because they were black Protestants and fodder for the devil.

His father slurps noisily at his cup. There is no sugar and Dave has learned to like his tea without it. His father, the hairy man, scratches at a column with a pencil, his tongue at the corner of his mouth.

'How did you sleep, lad?'

'All right.'

He lifts another huge page of the ledger and overturns it like a collapsing wall, the breeze of it sucking up a loose piece of paper. Dave watches it waft to the floor.

'Fetch that up for us will you please?'

Dave has been happy just to sit there, warm mug in his hands, thinking of nothing, but a father's word is law. He makes a dive for the paper. He will not be the half-wit with crumbs of sleep in his eyes. The piece of paper is an invoice.

Account sales of . . . . *14 Head Cattle*

Sold on. . . . . *28th April 1933*

By order and account of . . . . *Mr Fitzgerald*

By   *William Inglis & Sons Ltd.*

                         Fat Stock Salesmen

'More cows, Dad?' Dave asks.

'A baby needs her milk.'

Dave wonders do not the boy babies also need their milk? He lowers his nose into his mug almost touching the tea. What did the baby Jesus in His manger drink if not milk? And who provided it? He returns to the document. William Inglis (*and sons*) that was the important bit.

South British Building 28 O'Connell St. Sydney

	59 14–
Charges: *Commission, 2%*	*1 10–*
Yard dues	*7–*
Freight	
Unloading and Drafting	*6–*
Condemned Cattle Fund, 1%	*11 11*
Feed and Paddocking	*2 14 11*
Total	*56 19 1*

'Fifty-six pounds!'

'For which I give thanks to be able to pay,' says the hairy man scratching his hard whiskers, 'There's plenty of people going hungry these days, but they will not do without their milk.'

At least, thinks Dave, they are still asleep tucked up in their beds. His father, milk vendor, makes a sound like sandpaper with his cheek. He could whittle a block of balsa wood down to nothing in no time.

'Finish your tea and let's get cracking.'

They swill their tea and drain it. Their Adam's apples dance in their throats.

Humming, his father leans against the door of the shed, scraping mud out of the sole of his boot with a stick. Some mornings there is frost in the lane, fine and white like the mould that grows on an old tomato. The horse stands on smooth cobblestones snuffling into its nosebag. Dave looks at his father. He has the blasted stick between his teeth now like a cigar, like someone in a comic book. Dave unhooks the nosebag, notices a rheumy muck seeping from the resigned, hollow eyes of the horse. A waxy tear frozen on its cheeks. Can horses cry? Were there horses on Calvary?

They each vault up into the seat.

'Leave room for your guardian angel, lad,' says his father.

(Mr Fitz *and son*) and they set off for the dairy.

The horse is at its most sprightly for the first ten minutes while the cart is empty. They clip along at a nice pace. Soon enough it slows down to its usual dawdle. There is something comforting about the soft clop of its hooves along the road. A pale flush on the horizon draining the dark out of the sky. The eastern stars towards Coogee and Randwick slowly going out like votive candles lit during the night to keep watch.

They ride in silence, until at last the father turns to the boy beside him.

'I take it you went to confession yesterday, son? About that matter we discussed.'

Dave nods, staring at the horse's rump.

'That's the ticket. I'll chat to Brother Maloney, and then no more shall be said about it. We want no more of them monkey shines.'

'Yes, Dad.'

Dave realizes, perhaps for the first time that his father probably feels as awkwardly about this as he has been made to feel. Like that strange business about being careful of Protestant girls, not that he has ever talked to a Protestant girl. Dave understands that it is his youth which is at fault. He doesn't know enough. That penance is as natural as breathing. They listen to the iron wheels grind along the road.

The cart moves much slower when it is full. The shoulder muscles of the horse bulging like something a boy might peruse before the privacy of his own mirror, and repent of the vanity afterwards. The horse meanders through the early morning streets while Dave and his father jog from cart to house and back carrying their jingling milk racks. Sometimes there is a woman waiting with a kind smile of thanks. Sometimes a man scurries out after they have passed and shovels up the horse's droppings for his garden. Dave does one side of the street, his father the other. Atkins, Poole, Lalor, Flemming, O'Leary, Divola, Killom, all the rest. The horse must know the names as well as Dave. People sometimes leave money in their milk box and Dave drops it—clink—into the leather pouch about his waist. Even if there is no money, and they know that the people cannot pay, Mr Fitz will still leave a pint, or a ladleful from the big urn, scooped out for unbrushed, sheepish looking mothers. Even the Protestant babies need their milk. He has a song, which he yodels out now and then when the horse turns into a new street.

'Milk for the bay-be

Cream for the lay-de.'

People say he has a nice tenor voice from practising in choir. Dave thinks it is just a loud voice. He is glad it is so early so not too many people can hear him. Sometimes his yodel makes dogs bark. Occasionally ladies come out in their dressing gowns and talk to him, comment on the dawn and its portents.

In Cumberland St, Dave notices that the horse is limping slightly. Examining the hoof, he finds a piece of broken dinner plate or something stuck in the soft part. He pulls it out gently. The horse jerks its leg, like Dave being woken up with the marsh-men of his dream and his father's cold hands on his feet. His father comes jogging back to the cart—he always gets so far ahead.

'What have you done to it?'

'She was limping.'

'Leave her alone and get a wriggle on. If you're late for school Brother Maloney will set the strapper on you.'

It's not me that makes me late, Dave thinks, it's that the legs that carry me are so tired.

'Lazy useless pieces of equipment,' Brother Maloney once hissed, swishing his cane against his calves for some venal misde-meanor. What did Dave need school for anyway? The sooner he set to work the better. The caning never upset him. It was only his body after all.

His father is already jogging up the road, carrying his rack of bottles. Certainly Brother Maloney will be in a savage mood if he is late again today. The horse has paused to rest by an old willow tree, its roots lifting up the cobblestones of the street. Dave looks at the piece of dinner plate or whatever it is. White with a blue design on it, and a speck of the horse's blood. How would a dinner plate get out here in the street? He wipes the blood on his shirt. White and blue, Our Lady's healing colours. The horse watches

Dave go to the tree. For some pale, unformed reason he snaps a bare switch from it, returns to the cart. Milk cans and bottles jingle softly. The horse's flank tics in an isolated shudder. In the distance he can hear his father yodelling, then a shrill whistle for the cart. But the horse is waiting for the tongue-clicking order. Dave can see a picture of Brother Maloney's face, his bamboo cane. Swish.

He crouches beside the cart.

Sometimes, when you have finished your boiled egg for dinner, you can turn the empty shell upside down in your eggcup and you can fool the other people that you have not yet started your egg, or have been given another one. Then you can tap it with your spoon and crack the shell—see, hollow—and the joke will be on them.

Making his hand into a fist, an eggshell, Dave places it beneath the iron rim of the wheel. The horse waits for the order. With the willow switch in his other hand, Dave lashes at the ticking flank. The cart jolts forward. The wheel is silent for a second, then rumbles on, leaving the hand, a mangled spider on the road, bones in it broken like a box of chalk or an old eggshell. The shard of dinner plate also lies crushed on the road. In the distance, his father's faint voice:

'Milk for the bay-be.

Cream for the lay-de.'

A Handful of Water

Only the tourists ride the camels. A local, who does not want to be laughed at, rides a horse. This is what I tell the skinny Australian who comes to me with his ginger moustache and eyes ablaze. My name is Habibi Elali, I tell him, and my job (I do not tell him) is to get money from tourists. In all of Al Qahirah I am one of the best and the police direct many of their dupes to me. They have too much money and too little sense. It is what makes the hands of the clock go round.

Once my cousin Jalal Hzaife was bitten on the shoulder by a camel. It picked him up and shook him like a doll and ever since I have been wary of them. A horse is more better. The skinny Australian, whose name is Mr Daniher (Call me Kevin) from Hamilton Hill, looks foolish astride his spavined nag with his funny hat and tight jeans. He pays for me to arrange photos of himself with the horse and himself with the desert. I can tell he would really like to get a camel into the picture somewhere, but I cannot be bothered with dirty, smelly, biting camels, animals that are imported, by and largely, from Australia.

The horse doesn't like Mr Kevin. It fidgets as if the sand is too hot for its hooves. It appears to be looking around for a means of scraping him off, but I place my palm over her nose and give her a *gurfa* of water from the cup of my hand. He tells me that my English is very good. I tell him thank you, mate, I learned from television and English tourists. See, I have him in the palm of my fist as, on that first morning, I escort him through the markets looking for magic carpets and Ali Baba lamps or whatever it is he thinks he might find.

Mr Kevin likes it that I call him mate. I can also talk like a tickety-boo sort of chap too, eh what, if it pleases me. If the dupe requires it.

Call me Kev, he says, but I cannot bring myself to do this. He is younger than I and it is such a silly sounding name. Mr Kevin tells me he has come to Egypt with a single purpose in mind. Perhaps I can help him achieve this purpose? Perhaps I can, I reply. He tells me he has sold his car in order to be able to afford this adventure, this pursuit of his singular purpose. Anyone who can afford to sell a car for profit can afford to sprinkle a little of it my way. And my brother Wassim's way. And my cousin Jalal the taxi driver's way. And the police sergeant Ravi Elassaad from Al Jizah, his way also.

So, looking authentic in his tight pants, I take the skinny Australian on his skinny horse over the Giza Plateau towards the pyramids. We spend half a day riding around each one, marvelling at their immensity. Yes, I coo encouragingly, marvel at their mighty immensity. To be honest I am a little jaded with the pyramids. Having grown up with them they are like the warts on the back of my hand, always there, like a cathedral, or a water fall, or an opera house might be to locals in other countries. Blasé I think is the word, but then it might be another word.

The Australian pays my brother Wassim (although he does not know we are brothers) fifty Egyptian pounds to lead us up the smallest pyramid. When we are one quarter of the way up the police sergeant Ravi Elassaad with a loud hailer orders us to come back down. He could be saying anything as far as Mr Kevin is concerned, all he has to do is sound like we are in trouble, like he will let us off this time. He shakes his finger. I translate the trouble we are in, and explain the dangers, not least of which are a hefty fine and perhaps a night in a Cairo dungeon. It is enough. Mr Kevin gazes wistfully over at his desired goal, his singular purpose. He has come all this way from Hamilton Hill to climb the Great Pyramid. The hook is baited. So far things are working out hunky dory.

It is illegal, I tell him, to climb the Great Pyramid. Unless—

Unless? he asks.

Unless you know the right people.

Do you know the right people, Habibi?

But of course.

How much will it cost?

Money is of no importance. It is the Great Pyramid.

The next day I wait for him to emerge from the lobby of the Sesame Hotel, (always open). The morning is raw and bright.

Mr Kevin, Mr Kevin, I call, crossing the street before any of the touters can accost him. I lead him to a good, cheap food stall where he can partake of a satisfying collation. (It has taken me a few hours with the phrase book to come up with this ruby). For a reasonable fee I offer him the perfectly legal adventure of walking around the second smallest of the pyramids. His expression is a sour one, as if he has bitten his tongue, but he agrees to follow me. He studies the granite casing stones, some still plastered in their white limestone, pondering the imponderable. How did the casing stones at the top of the pyramid, weighing approximately two hundred tones each, come to be placed there without the assistance of a crane or modern surveying equipment? Some people can never be satisfied with a mystery. They have to tickle and tease it into giving up its secrets. They have to reduce it. He asks what I think about the ramp theory. I shrug. It is what it is.

Do you subscribe then, Mr Kevin asks, to the idea of aliens?

No, I say, we built them.

We, Habibi?

My people.

I take him inside to the chambers with their granite coffins, precisely carved. He takes a small knife from his pocket and tries to insert it between two of the giant stones within the chamber.

See, he says, I can't even get the blade in so perfectly are they conjoined.

My memory of his exact words is not so completely faithful. Yes, yes, it's a common experiment. Aliens, hmph. I show him some graffiti scrawled by a circus strongman from Paris in the nineteenth century, but this is of little interest to an amateur

Egyptologist like Mr Kevin. We go out into the light. I offer to take him to the catacombs at Saqqara where there are four million mummified ibis to be admired and wondered at.He says that in Hamilton Hill an ibis is considered vermin.

Next we ride over to the Great Pyramid itself. We, or rather he, pays for a boy to mind our horses. We stand and look up at the monumental height. There are many tourists doing the same, their guides pointing out unique features of interest. Graffiti from the circus strongman usually earns me a few pounds. Mr Kevin is clearly not satisfied with merely standing at the bottom. He is itchy to scamper up it like a monkey. Had he done so he might have been instantly arrested and all my work unentangled. I lay my hand on his arm.

Be patient, like the Sphinx. I shall talk to someone with the power. It will be more better.

Westerners like it when you use expressions like: *Be patient, like the Sphinx.* Again Mr Kevin tries his mischief with the little knife, trying to insert the blade between the giant stones.

He says in a voice of amazement it is too perfect. It's like it's been made by machine. How did they achieve such feats of engineering with only brass saws and copper chisels? I don't care what anyone says, it would have been impossible to construct by hand.

I see Mr Kevin has also been busy with his guidebook.

I take him to the Red Pyramid and the Unas Pyramid in my cousin's taxi, but these do not impress him. He wants the real McCoy. Then I take him to the actual Sphinx about half a kilometer down the road. More coin passes hand as I take him in the back way through a hole in the fence so as to avoid the entry fee.

While walking around the Sphinx with a horde of other tourists Mr Kevin makes the acquaintance of two attractive Scottish girls with uncovered hair. They walk together, posing for photos, laughing. I am amazed that barely before they have introduced their names and country of origin, telephone numbers are exchanged. They do not pay much attention to the Sphinx.

The next day my services are not required and I think I have lost my fish. In anger I yell at my wife. To get back at me she puts pepper in the couscous. I keep my beady eye on Mr Kevin from Hamilton Hill. I observe distantly that, after a day at the Cairo museum, and browsing through markets, and an evening at a fancy restaurant the three infidels then spend a night drinking and carousing until all hours. I wonder why is it that infidels seem to have all the fun? I go home late and jaded and sleep not a wink.

I am not the only one. The following morning Mr Kevin, with heavy bags under his eyes, seeks me out in the shadows across the street. The street is empty but for some chickens. I could knife him now and relieve him of his wallet, no one would know. Or to be more better, no one would care.

I need to climb the Great Pyramid and I need to do it today, he says. My friends have invited me to Glasgow and I need to book a flight. Can you help me?

But of course. Today, however, is an impossibility. Meet me here at midnight.

And I walk off, my sandals slapping the ground. I am the one playing the hard to catch. Glasgow, Hamilton Hill, it is all right for some infidels. I go to do some other business. I visit my mother to take her some bandages and to see the police sergeant. To pull, as they say, a few strings, but I have never been quite certain how many is a *few*, and whether a few is enough.

All the other touters know by now not to go near my dupe. At midnight it starts to rain. Mr Kevin, looking forlorn, is waiting for me outside the hotel.

Does this mean we will have to postpone our climb?

Not at all, I say. This is a good omen. Baal is with us. Rain in Egypt is not so common. You are meant to climb. The omen, however, is an expensive one.

I tell him I will need money to grease the fingers of the police sergeant, the taxi driver, and the guide who will lead him to the top.

Who will be the guide? he asks.

Me.

The taxi takes us through some deserted back streets and bazaars. We reach the vast fence surrounding the Plateau of Giza. Mr Kevin pays the taxi driver, (more, I note, than he has earned in a month). We go through the hole in the fence. Fortunately, tonight, no one else has the same idea. We creep past numerous tombs slick with rain, weeping statues of Anubis and Thoth. We move past them, through the dark. We walk for nearly half an hour, all the while before us the darker silhouette of the pyramid dominating the night. Not too many people actually want to climb the pyramid, including me. I must, as I have read, grid my lions.

Luckily the rain stops just as we reach the foot of the first massive blocks. Instead there is a little wind. I decide to tell him about my sick mother and how I will not be able to accompany him after all, may the gods be with him, good luck. I turn as if to go.

Wait.

He is prepared to pay another hundred pounds and I reluctantly accept. My fish has landed.

The rocks decrease in size as we ascend. There is a method to it: a lifting of one leg and a little hop with the other, like a small dog climbing up steep stairs. It seems to go on forever. After thirty minutes we are almost half way up. The Australian says he must rest. I wonder what I shall do if he has a heart attack way up here, or if some other accident should alas befall him. We take further breaks the higher we climb. Nearer the top, the rocks return to their previous enormity.

Why did they bring such large rocks to the top? Mr Kevin asks, teasing the mystery into a little irksome sore in his brain. They had no cranes, and any ramp this high would have had to stretch all the way to the horizon. Even the idea of a circular ramp is ridiculous.

Westerners always make these observations.

In an hour we finally reach the top. Mr Kevin rests, breathing hard. He lies down on the stone. He drains his bottle of water with no thought for the future. Then he stands up and faces all four points of the compass and stretches out his arms. The city lights wink below us. He clasps his hands together and appears to meditate upon his situation, or perhaps it is called praying? He is not even facing Mecca. He takes a few photographs and I am sure the flash from his camera can be seen across all the city. I eat some currants, sip a handful of water.

The size of a 42-story building Habibi, he says, can you imagine it? They could not have carried stones so heavy this high. They could not.

I have never seen a 42-story building, apart from on television, apart from this one we are standing on. I tell him it is time to go down. He refuses.

Just a little longer, he breathes deeply, dream of a lifetime.

I repeat my request several times. My sweat has cooled and the wind is making me shiver.

Mr Kevin, I say, we must go. The fines are insurmountable. And my mother is lying ill in her bed.

Just five more minutes.

If we are caught by the police in daylight it will be more worse for us.

I've come all this way, he says, I'm not going down yet.

To delay, I say, will cost one hundred more pounds.

He pays without a murmur.

He says, Money is of no importance, it is the Great Pyramid.

I feel the dagger tied with string to my leg and wonder if I can use it to negotiate a further fee for the descent. Allah would not begrudge me. But before I can Mr Kevin takes the remaining hundred-pound notes from his wallet—

No!

—and flings them into the air, where the breeze distributes them down the south-eastern slope of the pyramid, tumbling them along, further, down, away, like leaves, like a *gurfa* of water through an open hand. I want to leap after them, but—

No.

I am aghast. Gone. All is gone.

I can wait no longer. In fury I begin my descent and he follows me. He must follow me. I hope he falls. The rain begins again. The stones are slippery. It is almost harder going down than coming up. One must lean back and slide over the lip of each stone like an eel. All the way down Mr Kevin mutters to himself. He mutters about a dream come true, first two women at the same time and now this.

Where is glory? I ask myself. Where is wonder? Surely Allah would not begrudge me a little knife in his kidneys.

It is nearly dawn when we reach the bottom. There are five policemen waiting for us, including my friend Ravi Elassaad from Al Jizah. They do not want to arrest us. There would be too much paperwork. It is clear all they want is money.

Mr Kevin brushes them aside saying, No more money. I've given it all to the guide. Touch me and I'll complain to the Embassy. I'll create a diplomatic incident. Translate that, Habibi. Tell them.

No, I say, the pyramid has the money, he gave it to the pyramid.

Mr Kevin heads past the crying tombs towards the distant hole in the fence, while the five policemen slowly turn to me for their cut.

I watch him go. Perhaps it's not too late. Perhaps I can get Ravi to stab him? But that is too great a favour. The rising sun licks at the wet stone, as Mr Kevin grows smaller, gliding away as if his feet do not quite touch the ground. The inscrutable mystery of the pyramids towers over us as the police and I divide our plunder six ways. Our families will all eat well tonight. In the distance, as the city wakes, the braying of a camel.

White to the End of the World

1.

Sure, shopping is an important part of life, but so are the 'relationships' you're 'supposed' to have with 'other people'. It's just that the relationships I seem to be having with other people are a fairly fragile prospect, especially if those involved are from another planet, or another generation entirely. And boy do they like to get involved.

In his hay-day Grandpie Errol, as I call him, worked as a scientist. What sort of a scientist, I'm not sure. Science is such a fuzzy thing. He retired twenty years ago so I guess that means he has had a good twenty years of not being a scientist, although he tells people he still has an interest in things that are 'scientific'. Cures for diseases and holes in the ozone layer and that sort of thing.He is still a member of the Royal Sciences Club. When they were younger my Grandpie and Grandmoo (as I call them) used to go there for what were called 'dinner dances'. One day I hope an anthropologist will explain the ritual significance of the 'dinner dance'.

I am fourteen. It seems I have been fourteen forever. I have my own life. Visiting my grandparents with their smells and yellow toenails and bandages does not figure greatly in it. They get bruised quite easily. Even bumping into furniture will bruise them, and they are always doing that. Their house is like a cross between a hospital, a crèche, and a mausoleum, what with the walking frames and hand rails in the shower and photos of people from the past all over the place. It is all I can do to be nice, but I am, because they are the parents of my mother. In the diplomacy of 'parent/child relations' it's advantageous to be on the good side of the mother. She's the one who controls the purse strings after all.

One day my father comes to me with a stern expression on his face, one of those indecipherable expressions that speak of the impossibility of knowing the depth of feeling inside another person. There, that doesn't sound like a fourteen year old speaking, does it. That sounds more like a text book. I suppose I am good at things not scientific. Waffling, for instance. He says that Grandpie Errol wants to have words with me.

'What for?' I protest. 'What have I done?'

'Nothing,' says my dad. 'It's a good thing. I think.'

'Then why do you look so angry?'

'I'm not angry at you, Denise.'

'Then what?'

'It's an in-law thing.'

So I get on the phone and talk to Grandpie. This is what he says: He says that he's been a member of the Royal Sciences Club for over sixty years. He says that as such a loyal member they have offered him and others like him first dibs on the adventure of a lifetime. Do I understand him? The adventure of a lifetime.

Already I am starting to feel a little bored. Also suspicious. What has this to do with me? I think back to the time when Grandpie deliberately let the battery in his electric wheelchair run down while he was on his way back from the shops, and then expected me to push him all the way home. As Mum explained, he may well have thought it might be an endearing moment between grandfather (him) and granddaughter (me) to give him a push up the hill. But it wasn't. It was revolting. I said to Mum there's no way I'm pushing that gross old man up the street where everyone could see me. Instead we went and got him in the car. That was a while ago now and I have learnt to swallow my pride. The flat battery was probably just a mistake.

Grandpie says the Sciences Club are going to charter a 747 and fly to Antarctica before it all disappears. How about that?

'That sounds great Grandpie,' I say.

'Yes. I've already bought the ticket.'

'Well, don't forget to take a scarf.'

'Not so fast, Missy.'

He explains that one clause of the insurance policy states that he has to have a 'check-up'. Well that's sensible. You don't want to send a bunch of geriatrics off to bob-sleigh across the Antarctic if they're not up to it. A little bit of a turnabout for them because they insured Grandpie, an octogenarian mind you, against breaking a hip and he's broken his hip three times, so he's quite cocky about having made a profit out of them.

He explains that he's already had his check-up and guess what?

'What?'

'The doctor said no.'

The doctor said he (Grandpie) was too frail and doddery on his pins to fly all that way. His dodgy heart and clapped out hips.

'Bad luck,' I say.

I am not sure that 'doddery on his pins' is a proper medical phrase. It is amazing to think of all the things that are wrong with him, not least of which would be his yellow toenails, and yet to see how optimistic he still is. He says that he is going to hang on to every scrap of life by his fingertips, a statement which gets my father rolling his eyes.

Then he says: 'Denise, I want you to be my proxy.'

'Your *what?*'

'I want you to go in my place. There's no rule against it.'

'I don't have a passport.'

'Irrelevant,' he barks. 'You don't need one.'

'But Grandpie,' (I'm trying to remember my manners here) 'I don't want to go to Antarctica.'

'Too late she cried,' he cries, 'the ticket's already been transferred into your name.'

Well . . .

This is what I mean about some people wanting to become involved in other peoples' business. I don't say that I'd rather go shopping for shoes in Bangkok. I don't say Nice is nice this time of year. I sigh to the bottoms of my socks. My mum shrugs sympathetically. If Antarctica is all there is on the table then I guess Antarctica will have to do. That is if you're in the not-looking-a-gift-horse-in-the-mouth sort of department. You wouldn't want him to waste his money. After I get off the phone my dad says he is not happy for me, a mere fourteen year old girl, to traipse off to Antarctica all by herself. A part of me wonders if he is the one who really wants to go and this is some sort of by-play between father-in-law and son-in-law. 'Politics' again.

'She won't be by herself,' says Mum. 'She'll be with a plane load of responsible people. All members of the Sciences Club.'

'Strangers,' says Dad. 'Traipsing off to Antarctica with a plane full of strangers.'

He really likes that word 'traipsing'.

'Responsible people,' continues Mum, 'like my father. I don't see why you're so set against it.'

'I'm not set against it,' says Dad. 'It's just that—that if anything should happen . . . if anything . . . I'd never forgive myself. I'd also never forgive him.'

I am astonished at this—my father actually feeling something.

'It's all right, Dad. I can look after myself.'

'It's the chance of a lifetime,' says Mum. She thinks Grandpie is hoping I might be bitten by the 'scientific bug' and follow a 'career' in science like him when really all I want to do is go shopping.

I say, 'I hope there's a vaccination for that bug.'

However, it seems my opinions don't count for much here.

2.

So, driven by Mum, I turn up at the airport at the appointed time on the appointed date. I am the youngest passenger on 'Special Flight 871' to Antarctica by about fifty years. Luckily there is a flight steward called Alan who tells Mum he will look after me, which is rubbish because as soon as we're on board and the door sighs shut, it is crystal clear that all the old scientists are in much greater need of being looked after than me.

We find our seats and everyone is settled. We are shown how to place an oxygen mask over our faces should the need arise. There is a lot of 'chit-chat' as the scientists talk excitedly to each other, like kids on an excursion to the museum.

Seated beside me is another octogenarian who introduces himself as Mr Scott.

'No relation,' he says.

I don't know what he means by this so I don't say anything.

'But you can call me Scotty.'

Scotty, apart from being an octogenarian, also used to be a Meteorologist and that is why for him this is the trip of a lifetime.

I don't say anything again.

'And to make it even more special I find I am seated next to a lovely young lady,' (me) 'from—where did you say you were from again?'

'I didn't.'

He has liver spots on his hands and scalp. His eyelashes are ginger. His ears are enormous. And wrinkled. And dandruffy. I locate the location of my sick bag, just in case. I examine the card showing the emergency exits. I am polite and tell Scotty the story of Grandpie Errol who wasn't allowed to come and wanted me to be (I hate to say it) his poxy. Scotty says that his doctor also told him he shouldn't come, but he (Scotty) insisted. The trip of a lifetime.

We take off, pushed back into the (upright) seats by the G-Force. Our ears pop as we ascend. We settle in for the flight. Luckily there is a movie channel on the screen in the back of the chair in front of me and I am able to tune out from the buzz of all the scientific beeswax. Scotty watches a documentary about leopard seals. He chats to the fellow across the aisle from him. When we reach our cruising altitude a voice comes over the loudspeaker:

'This is Captain Malone ... welcome aboard flight 871 to Antarctica ... *(crackle, crackle)* ... seat belt sign has now been switched off ... *(crackle, crackle)* ... hope you enjoy your flight ... *(crackle, crackle, pop)* ... refreshments ... *(pop, pop)* ... sit back and ... *(pop)* ...'

I put the buds back in my ears. Soon all the scientists are being given complimentary champagne. Alan looks twice at me before, sadly, shaking his head.

Six hours is an awfully long time to sit on a plane, only to find when you get there you have to turn around and come back, (which may explain why I didn't need a passport). A smattering of rain slides horizontally across the window. To avoid thrombosis I get up and pace up and down the aisles, but it is awkward and embarrassing clambering over Scotty, so once I am seated I try to stay put. I pretend to go jogging on the spot. To avoid thrombosis Scotty shows me his pressurised socks. Luckily I have also brought a book which I have read before so I know it will be interesting. Instead of champagne, Alan brings me a cup of tea. Another gift-horse. We all eat our sandwiches.

After a couple of hours I note there is quite a bit of heavy-duty napping going on. Just like Grandpie in front of the fire. I hope that this is not going to be another of those mysterious flights that disappears off the radar without a trace. That would be just dandy, to vanish off the face of the earth with no one for company but all these liver-spotted, wrinkly-eared scientists. Captain Malone tells us that below and to the starboard side is Heard Island. Everyone on the starboard side looks out their windows while everyone on the other side misses out. I guess they'll see it on the way back. I think about telling Scotty an Antarctic joke—that I have never 'heard' of Heard Island, but I think it might give him the wrong impression, that I am trying to be friendly or something.

After what feels like about a quarter of my lifetime, an announcement comes over the PA that if we look out the windows now we might see icebergs. There is a flutter of excitement. Our first icebergs. There is another rush for the windows. Really, they're behaving like children. I guess it's lucky there are no clouds today—no refunds for overcast Antarctic weather conditions. Having a window seat is not such a good idea now because Scotty keeps leaning over my shoulder, breathing on me, to get as close to the view as possible. He offers me his binoculars, but I decline.

There are certainly icebergs. From this height they must be the size of shopping malls. Then they start to thicken into sea ice where the dark sea laps at the chipped edges, like maps of strange countries, or the veins on old saucers in antique shops. Then, the further south we go, they join up into matted blankets of white.

The scientists are on cloud nine going back and forth from 'starboard' to 'port'. (It takes me a while to work out which is which.) I even take a few photos out the window for Grandpie with my phone.

White, all white to the end of the world.

The scientists are all as happy as Larry, whoever Larry was. My ears pick up a jumble of strange phrases.

Leaning over my shoulder, Scotty mutters more to himself than to me, 'Amery ice shelf . . . Murray monolith . . . Scullin monolith . . . Enderby land . . . Proclamation Island . . . Moldezhnaya . . . Unbelievable . . .'

All I see is ice. Scotty tells me that it is so cold down there that if you threw a bucket of boiling water into the air it would freeze by the time it hit the ground. Then the plane starts to descend low over the ice mass. Lower and lower. No one told me that we were going to land. I start to worry that this is it: this is where we disappear off the radar screen. Why isn't anyone smashing down the pilot's door?

'We are now cruising at 1500 metres above the ice,' says Captain Malone.

The plane skates above the ice, all the scientists going, 'My goodness,' and 'Holy moley.' Then it starts to climb again. When we are high enough the plane banks to the right and we start to head home.

Is that it? I say to myself. Is that all? All this way and not a single penguin. No one seems to be concerned that we have brought a plane load of ozone depleting greenhouse aviation gases up really close to the hole they are all so worried about. At least I know that much. I turn to voice my opinion to Scotty, but he's fallen asleep again. No one else seems to be disappointed. In fact they all seem to be as chuffed as monkeys—exhausted and exhilarated. Maybe there's something I am missing.

Eventually we leave the white nothingness behind, then the fractured sheet ice, then the icebergs thinning out, becoming fewer in the ink of the ocean far below. Nothing but the sea's flat rag. And there's still six hours to go.

In time Alan comes around again with his trolley of nuts and wine in tiny bottles. I ask for champagne but he gives me a can of soft drink instead like I'm a kid or something.

'Mr Scott would you care for a Merlot?'

Scotty doesn't answer.

'Mr Scott?'

Alan gives Scotty a curious prod and all he (Scotty) does is lean slowly towards me, the binoculars still around his neck, until gravity takes hold and he slumps all his weight against me. He knocks the soft drink out of my hand. His gross head is on my boob.

'Hey.'

I shove him away with my elbow. Alan takes a step backwards. Then he puts his fingers to the pulse in Scotty's neck, only there isn't one. Nor is there one in his wrist. He's stopped breathing. Alan shakes Scotty vigorously. Nothing, except his glasses fall off. Alan looks at me and that's when I start screaming because the weight of this old man is all over me and his ears are wrinkled and no one is telling me what is going on.

Another flight attendant comes and they manage to dig me out from under Mr Scott, who is as loose as a puppy, or a balloon full of oil. I see at close quarters that Mr Scott has kicked off his shoes. A yellow toenail protrudes from a hole in his pressurised sock. Finally they take me to a spare seat at the back of the plane where I can dry my eyes and 'compose myself'. I watch a crowd of people standing around Mr Scott's body, but there's not much they can do with it here on the plane.

'What's going on up there?' asks my new neighbour, but I say nothing. I just stare at the backs of my hands and count the freckles.

Apart from my photos I am supposed to give Grandpie Errol a 'Report on the Expedition'. It will be called 'Denise of the Antarctic'. I don't yet know what it will say. That there were no penguins. That Mr Scott had a hole in his sock. My conclusion: that I don't think I have been bitten by the 'science bug'. No fear, I've seen what can happen. Science didn't help Mr Scott. Not even a couple of guys in tight pants with a bit of first aid could help him. All those scientists and not a doctor among them.

It is a long trip back. People keep asking me if I am all right. I shrug and do not speak. I cannot watch the movie channel, (service temporarily disconnected). I cannot read my book, mainly because I have left it under Mr Scott's body and I don't ever want to touch it again. I don't even have a window to look out of anymore. Just the scientists all about me, discussing, mumbling, dozing, snoring. The captain's crackly voice says we are now over Tasmania, but it is dark outside now and you can't see anything. I feel I am the only one awake, as we return from the pole, the last one left.

Morris Minors

My mother has asked me on a date. I suppose you could call it a date. An outing. That's better. It is kind of quaint, and also kind of not.

My mother is a painter; what the cynics call a weekend painter. Little old lady paintings I call them, which is unfair, because she's been doing it for decades and still makes a bit of money. Watery landscapes mainly; still lives and so on, although recently she has branched out into charcoal. The tonal realist school, if you want a label.

Being December, today is the day her painting group is having their Christmas party and she has asked me to accompany her. Why not? It's not normally a time of year I would be here, living interstate as I do, but tomorrow is the funeral of my aunt who has died after a long illness, and so I am here, out of my comfort zone, doing the right thing. I am surprised that in the space of a page a simple event like Christmas drinks has already become inordinately complicated. In the days leading up to the funeral life is carrying on. There is no reason why it shouldn't. However, life carrying on in the small town where my mother lives carries on in slow motion. It is like watching the tendril of a new leaf unfurl, or a whale playing chess.

The aunt is not my mother's sister. *Was,* sorry, *was.* She was my mother's sister-in-law. They did not get on, and have managed to maintain this grudge for fifty years. I have never really understood why. My mother felt possessive about her brother Steve, who died long ago. I remember my uncle. He was the one who taught me how to play draughts and do somersaults on the lawn. There are photos of him, strong and bare-chested, with kids balancing on his shoulders. One of those kids is me. I even remember the muscles in his back.

My mother was close to Steve, by all accounts. When the end came for him they all sat about his bedside, but he was too dosed up on morphine to know who was there. I guess it's a common story. After a while the nurses sent everyone outside. Some messy business to be performed. Out in the corridor my mother suddenly stopped, pretended she had left something behind, then ducked back into the room. Behind the curtain she placed her hand on Steve's arm and his eyes opened. They looked at each other. She gave his arm a squeeze, realizing she was never going to see him again.

I must have been nearly thirty when this happened.

Steve's children, my cousins, I knew better when we were little. Now I only ever see them at funerals. There have been the funerals of their father, my brother, an old patriarch on someone's side of the family. Maybe one or two others. My cousins are the sort of people I now only ever have cause to meet at funerals. In that respect, which is rather Pavlovian, I always think of them as very well dressed people. People that I have unfortunately come to associate with death. Tomorrow it is their mother's turn.

In the years following my uncle's passing I occasionally find my mother sitting in a darkened room listening to something classical, and know she is thinking of her brother. This is a melancholy picture. I feel the torpor of a son's responsibility. What should I do? She is starting to forget things, but so do I for that matter. Anyway it's only small things. Alternately she remembers things I would rather she didn't. Things I said when I was little; things that happened when she was young. The Miss Elcinous drawer, for instance, is a long standing joke. It took me a long time to work out that she was referring to a drawer full of *miscellaneous* odds and ends. I always understood, and this is the joke, that the drawer belonged to a person called Miss Elcinous. What she forgets is that she has told me this story, and others like it, over and over again and I have to pretend that I am hearing it for the first time.

A whale playing chess.

I have no strong feelings about my aunt. I remember her laughing at something I had done once that I did not think was funny. I guess I have to side with my mother in this rivalry. We are born bearing grudges, and my mother has now lost hers.

So I drive her to Christmas drinks, with all the painting ladies. Life carrying on. A leaf unfurling. There are eighteen of them.

They all cluck over me as I am introduced. One of them even films me saying 'hello' with her mobile phone. Over the course of lunch several of them reveal that they know more about me than I know about them. I know nothing about them. My mother has obviously been talking. I am polite. I eat what they offer. It is nice to see that she has friends. I am surprised to see she is so popular.

'Have you tried the blue jelly?'

I eat some blue jelly. There is also mushroom quiche and asparagus fingers and toasty things and cake. I make the right noises.

'Have you seen the cars? You must get Ern to show you the cars.'

Ern, the husband of Joan, who is hosting Christmas drinks, collects Morris Minors. Being the only two males amongst the eighteen painting ladies it seems entirely proper that I ask about the cars and that Ern show them to me. It also seems proper that the women should shoo us off to do this. Ern jumps up. The painting ladies are starting to get the giggles. The corks are popping. It's looking to be a long lunch. We'd best scamper. Outside I note there are goldfish in the pond by the door. That's interesting.

Ern leads me down the yard to his shed. It is a custom built edifice made from second hand materials designed to make it look older than it actually is. There is an antique petrol bowser out the front to lend an air of verisimilitude. I have never seen such a neat looking shed. Inside, after he turns on the lights, I count eighteen cars shrouded under white, canvas covers. I ponder the coincidence of there being eighteen painting ladies inside as well as eighteen shrouded Morris Minors out here. At least I presume they are Morris Minors. Ern unhooks the cover of one and flicks it back with a practised hand. Under it is a Morris Minor.

'This was my first car. 1953,' he says proudly.

It is a shiny and blue. Immaculate—that is the word they use about cars. Immaculate condition. As new. Shiny as the duco on a coffin.

'I sold it when our third child came along, then when my son turned eighteen he reminded me that I'd promised this car to him, so we tracked down the lady I sold it to, living up in the Mallee she was, and bought it back at a slight markup but not too terrible.'

I understand that Ern really likes his Morris Minors, although I don't know why he thinks it is important for me to know this story.

He unwraps another. And another. One is lavender. One has smooth wooden panels. One is an actual Morris Minor police car imported from England, circa 1971, with POLICE stenciled along the sides and a siren that, after hooking it up to a battery with silver terminals, blares out loudly. There is even a bobby's helmet and truncheon sitting on the front seat. Ern is in his element. I ask him a number of car related questions. How long has he been collecting them? Which is his favourite? How much are they worth? Strangely I can't recall the answers to these questions. I am the sort of person who regards a car to be an inanimate machine intended to transport me from point A to point B. It should not have a personality. I do not care that they are shiny, or lavender. However, I much prefer this conversation to what I might expect inside with the painting ladies where they would probably ask me about myself.

I probe Ern with a few more mechanical questions and he starts to fly, describing the history of the Morris Minor, its place in cultural consciousness. He also likes Chevrolets, but it is the Morris Minor that is his passion. His talk falters. Suddenly it becomes clear that Ern doesn't want to tell me anymore about his collection. Perhaps he has given too much away. I suppose he presents this talk to more important people than me. I suppose he might even charge money for it. He wants to wrap them all up again and lock the door. I help him do this. He waddles back up towards the house.

Outside, under a tree, I note five more Morris Minors, all rusty old bombs covered in lichen. Future projects, I am guessing, or else cadavers farmed for spare parts. I take a look around the garden. Also immaculate—there, I see I am wrong about that word. Nevertheless it is still an awful word.

I stop and study the goldfish. A cigarette butt floats among the lilies. I wipe my feet. I go inside to all the laughter.

'Have some blue jelly. There's plenty of blue jelly.'

I have some blue jelly, even though I don't like it. I begin to see that my mother has a life beyond any that I suspected her of having. I find this a profound relief. It suddenly feels like something I am not expected to provide.

After a while we say our goodbyes. Ern has disappeared. No solidarity there. My mother rinses her empty plate. I put her in the car and chauffer her home, careful not to drive too fast. Chopin is playing on the radio and she tells me again how her own mother used to love playing Chopin; she was a fine concert pianist. Another story I have heard before. It may well be true.

47

She remembers we have a funeral to go to tomorrow. Her sister-in-law, with whom she never really got on. She thinks about
what to wear. I will no doubt see my cousins again. I realise, with
a jolt of shock, that if my cousins have come to represent death
for me, strange collocation, then I probably foreshadow the same
for them. I am the portent of grief and sorrow. We are reciprocal
omens. Gee. Here I am trying to do the right thing when all along
I have been the harbinger of death. When they see me the scythe
shall be unsheathed and the harvest struck down. Death will walk
the land in my shadow. Perhaps I am being melodramatic. There
is no way to clear up this misperception without actually talking
to my cousins about it. They'll be upset. There'll be tears. I don't
know if I am up to it, nor if the actual funeral is the right time
and place.

Afterwards I will go home. But all that is tomorrow. There is a
whole evening to get through yet. On the drive back to the town
where my mother lives I note how full the dams are, how green
the paddocks, the moon in the sky white as a tooth.

'I hope you weren't too bored,' she says, nursing her handbag.

'It was fine. Those cars were interesting.'

On the radio Chopin does his business.

Then she says, 'Did you ever meet my brother?'

I do a double-take, hands on the wheel.

'What?'

'My brother, Steve. He died years ago. Did you ever meet him?'

The fence posts flash by. I don't really know how to respond
to this question, so I close my mouth and just focus on the road.

My Father's Shopping List

The trouble with having a doctor for a father is that you are brought up calling a spade a spade. Or more accurately a spatula a spatula, a scalpel a scalpel. There is no room for subtlety. You couldn't, in our house call a hypodermic syringe a 'needle' and get away with it. I was forever being reminded that hearts pump blood, they don't *break* and they don't feel sorrow. You couldn't call an egg whisk a whisker, nor could you call a test tube that glass thingy where the sperm and the egg were mixed so that some kind of conjunction might occur. No. Right term for the right instrument, that was my father's edict. Especially in Woy Woy, where he was trying to raise me above the lowest common denominator. The trouble with having a doctor for a father is that you have to call everything by its proper name.

Every structural part, every bodily function had its own proper title. These I have inculcated from an early age. When

I was but five years old, for instance, in grade-one, I raised my hand to ask if I could go to the toilet. A common enough, simple enough request, and one I had been trained for.

'Yes Lauren, what is it?' asked Miss York.

However the words that came out of my mouth were, 'I need to micturate some urine.'

Silence.

Perhaps I had breached a matter of grade one etiquette? Perhaps I had mixed up the noun and the verb? No one in the room knew what I was talking about, not even Miss York, whom I loved and would never have wanted to be rude to.

I soon learned there were two languages. One for ordinary, everyday things such as *saucepan, butter knife, carrot,* and another, proper language of which my father approved. Since my mother's death in my infancy my father was the only one to do any approving in my life. It was a miserly currency. How far did I go out of my way to seek this? If I grazed my knee in the playground—no, no, I grazed my *patella*—I would explain to Miss York as she placed a band-aid on the wound. I also sometimes wondered whether or not I hurt myself on purpose so she might tend to me.

I did not chew my lunch, I masticated. I did not burp, I eructated. Soon enough I learned the perils of this second language. Miss York advised me to develop the habit of thinking before speaking. Of keeping mum. Scorn and frank disdain became my lot. Ostracism also. If it wasn't for Hilary, my best friend, no, my only friend, I wouldn't even have known I had so many nicknames. *Smartarse,* for one, *Rudolf,* (as in having my nose in the air) for another, and *Mickey* (as in micturate). It is hard to live these things down. My father told me not to bother with them. They were plebeians.

'Even Hilary?'

'Even Hilary.'

Hilary's father was an Anglican minister, so she was about as popular as me.

These events were so humiliating I resolved to never speak in the discourse of my father other than in his presence, when I wanted his praise, or some other currency. This came in handy whenever he had to compose a shopping list (he had a doctor's handwriting) and I was able to scribe for him.

'We need something with a good balance of carbohydrate, sodium, sugars and protein.'

'You mean Corn Flakes, Dad.'

'Yes, yes. That's the stuff.'

I became his translator, whereas Hilary taught me the common argot of the schoolyard, which I can't bring myself to repeat here as I was the brunt of so much of it. In this manner I grew. *Schoolbus, homework, chalk* and so on.

As one of the rare GPs of Woy Woy my father delivered a good deal of the babies born in the district. Many of the local women therefore thought he was wonderful, or more colloquially, they thought the sun shone out of his trousers. He was often on call at the hospital which serviced the clutch of small surrounding towns. As such he was a local identity. This was in the days before the era of home birthing, or even the now common presence of the progenitor—see, it's a hard habit to break, this seeking my father's approval—in the delivery room.

One day my progenitor arrived home tired and cranky. The latest baby had kept him waiting. Dystocia. I had learned to cook from a young age and I presented him with a cheese and gherkin sandwich. I must have been home on my own, for I can't recall anyone looking after me, guiding my hand holding the breadknife. After eating it, he bundled me into his car, a Valiant Chrysler, and drove to a strange house only a few minutes away. It was dark. He piggy-backed me down the path at the side of the house, past the garbage bins. There was a radio playing. He opened the gate and we went into the back yard. A light illuminated the kitchen window which was steamed over. Inside, a man stood at the sink. I could hear the clatter of plates and cutlery. Perhaps it was only one plate. Dad went up close and told me to knock on the window. I did.The man gave a start, shielding his eyes so as to be able to see out into the darkness. He rubbed clear a circle in the steam. He saw me sitting on my father's back.

'Tim,' my father called out.

'Yes?' said the man called Tim. 'Is that Doctor Harrison?'

'Congratulations. It's a boy.'

'A boy?'

'Yes. A male. Six pounds three ounces.'

A slow smile spread across the man's face like welcome rain down a dry creek.

'And then look what happens,' he proffered me over his shoulder, shoving me into the light from the window. 'You can't stop them growing. They're like weeds. It's a jolly good game.'

My father carried me back through the gate, careful to close it behind us. He drove home and I wondered about this matter of another being entering the world and how such news is announced, welcomed, dreaded. I knew all about the various stages of gravidity and parturition, and how such conditions came about, but nothing about the emotions that accompanied these physical, transformative states. *Kneecap–patella; shoulder-blade–scapular; tummy ache–constipation.* But love? A heart does not *break,* nor does it feel sorrow. I grew up with this split vocabulary; with a painful awareness of euphemism. I had intuitions of emotion, but not the nomenclature to describe it.

Knowing the right terms did not necessarily prevent the blood rising in my cheeks, for example, as a symptomatic manifestation of embarrassment. Oh, I knew how to blush. I knew that it is euphemism that greases the social wheels. One of my adolescent names was the reverse of euphemism. I don't know if there is a term for this. As a pimply teenager my nickname amongst the boys, so Hilary told me, was *pus-face.* It put me off boys. Some things traverse this double life of language. Some words have a foot in both camps as it were, that transcend the limitations of either house. One of these is period pain. Another is penis pump.

When I left home and went to university in Sydney my father continued his work in Gosford, living in the satellite town of Woy Woy. Despite his popularity he never wanted to remarry. He just wanted to help people. I had long outgrown this town with its nicknames and abbreviations, and quiet sense of exclusion. As soon as I could I moved into student accommodation on campus, where I studied languages, majoring in German. Hilary was at the University of New South Wales, so we were able to catch up on weekends, if we felt like it. Childhood faded behind us and we did not miss it.

Apart from delivering babies my father had all the other attendant duties of a GP in a rural community. Every ailment under the sun. Midwives took over a lot of his business. I guess delivering news about another being coming into the world was one of the more pleasant of these duties, and I never forgot the smile that came over that man's face when Dad told him he had a brand new son. Another one was assisting people at the beginning of this process, namely engaging with issues of fertility. He appreciated the desperation with which some people wanted to have a baby.

One day he phoned me on the public phone in the foyer of the college dormitory. Someone had to come and find me. It saddens me to say I was doing nothing that I shouldn't have been. Without divulging patient confidentiality he said that one of his patients, a male if I must know, was having some difficulties with maintaining blood supply. Was this a euphemism? Maintaining blood supply? Was he a haemophiliac? Well, I thought, put a band-aid on it or else he might bleed to death. But no, I wasn't paying attention. In short, he wanted me, and I don't know how many other fathers have asked this of their daughters, to purchase a penis pump.

I had never heard of a penis pump before. I'd heard of a breast pump for busy, lactating mothers, or else to help ease painful mastitis, but a pump for a penis? What did that look like? Was it like a bicycle pump? So this was the conversation we were now having.

'Can't you buy your own penis pump, Dad?'

'It's not for me.'

'Who's it for?'

'I can't tell you that.'

'Is it for Mr Nemeth who works in the post office?'

'No.'

I could see I wasn't going to get anywhere with that gossipy line of enquiry.

'But Dad, I can't do that.'

'Why on earth not?'

'Well, because I'm a girl.'

'How many shops do you think sell penis pumps in Woy Woy?'

'How many sell them in Sydney?'

'Use your brain, Lauren. A sex shop. Go to a sex shop.'

My father is saying he wants me to go to a sex shop.

'You want me to buy you a sex toy?'

'Not a toy. An aid. A medical aid to help ameliorate an erectile dysfunction in an unfortunate patient who is suffering.'

(This was in the days before the medical miracle of Viagra.)

'Is it for Mr Carruthers, the baker?'

'No.'

'But Dad . . . '

'You will be fully reimbursed.'

'Well . . . '

'What's the problem here?'

'Well, I suppose I could do that.'

'Good girl.'

He had said the magic words.

'Is that all you want?' I thought I was going to have to make another shopping list.

'That's all for the moment.'

The next Sunday I met Hilary. I couldn't bring myself to go on my own. We caught the train to Kings Cross, heart of the red light district. Even though it was Sunday morning the pubs were doing a roaring trade. Juke box music poured from their doors. There were greasy looking spruikers outside the strip clubs, the Pink Pussycat, Les Girls, trying to drum up interest.

'Step this way ladies . . .'

Everyone on the street appeared hung-over, or as if they hadn't slept at all, and the party was still going on. There were needles in the gutter—no, not needles, hypodermic syringes. A man lay asleep on the footpath outside the railway station. He was so still he might have been dead. People stepped around him. You could have put a bomb under him and he wouldn't have budged. He certainly looked like he would have some trouble maintaining blood supply. Another man, wearing pyjamas, stood in the middle of the road directing traffic. Another fellow stood up to his knees in the floating dandelion of the El Alamein Fountain. A young girl with torn stockings, sat on an upside down milk crate outside a chemist. She was barely conscious, nodding to herself, listening to silent, opiate music. When you see these things you wonder if you are looking at lives that aren't going to be long ones. They all seemed to gravitate to the Cross. Other people singing at the tops of their voices. Mad people talking to themselves, frothing at the mouth. Even they had families somewhere; even they once had had childhoods and mothers who loved them. Where were their families now?

Physically it's only a relatively short journey from Woy Woy to the Cross, but they are worlds apart. Although we were aware of what went on in the red light district it wasn't every day that Hilary and I, being studious introverts, got to witness it first hand. There were several sex shops to choose from. We chose The Venus Love-In, which, for some reason, looked slightly more salubrious than the others, with names like The Love Muscle or Jungle Juice. Perhaps we were swayed by the pink lettering stencilled across the window, or the absence of bars over the glass, or the bright *XXXX* sign over the doorway. We went in, checking first to see if we'd been noticed by anyone we knew. There was no one we knew. We went up the stairs. Several seedy looking men stood, round shouldered, at racks of magazines and videos. (This was back in the days before the DVD and before, I should point out, the convenience of online purchasing.) The shop was bristling with erotica, is that the correct term? Several technical phrases sprang to mind. There was a predominance of leather, and I don't mean beige.

'Look at those whips,' Hilary whispered in astonishment.

Right at eye level, there in front of us, was a display of magazines. On the cover of one was the picture of a young man who looked like he was having a nice time relaxing in the sun, working on his tan, except that he had another man's arm, what could be seen of it, right up his bottom. Hilary's jaw was wide open in the colloquial language of shock. The magazine was called, in bold Germanic font—*After Faust*. That was calling a spade a spade, even if it was a German one. Hilary and I stared at each other. Was this real? Was this a part of the world we lived in?

'Ladies,' said the man behind the counter. 'How can I help you?'

In a glass display cabinet behind him was a dizzying array of dildos in all shapes and sizes.

We kept our eyes straight ahead; this seemed to be the safest course. All around were mannequins wearing a range of corsetry: crotchless knickers, nippleless bras, studs, masks, dog-collars. Coloured condoms blown up into dirigibles. We didn't know where to look.

'We would like to buy a penis pump,' I said, taking a breath. I tried to maintain the demeanour of a professional buyer after, perhaps, a trowel in the hardware section, as if it was something I ordered every day. Some of the dildos behind the man were *huge*. Others were *enormous*. At that moment I couldn't rightly tell the difference.

'Of course you do,' said the man, who looked profoundly bored. Even his slick moustache drooped in boredom.

'I don't,' said Hilary, distinguishing herself from our collective cause. 'She does.'

'It's for a medical procedure.'

'Hey, I'm not judging,' said the man. 'What colour?'

'Er . . . We don't mind.'

'They come in ebony, red, tiger-striped or flesh-coloured.'

'I really don't mind.'

'How about flesh coloured then?'

'Fine.'

The seedy men at the magazine racks were studying us now. Listening with intent. *After Faust* was still enjoying the sun. It was hard to look away. How was that physically possible?

'Now, what size?'

'I . . . er . . . I guess about average.'

'Good choice.'

The man disappeared through a plastic curtain to a store room out the back. We were left with an uninterrupted view of the cabinet of dildos. Hilary and I looked at each other again, struggling to keep our faces straight, on the verge of hysteria. Everywhere we looked there was something upright, protruding, gaping there in front of us. It was quite gynaecological. Soon he returned with an anonymous brown box.

'Do you want me to show you how it works?'

Hilary and I answered simultaneously.

'No.'

'Yes.'

'No, really it's not necessary,' I said.

'Well, would you like it gift-wrapped?'

'No.'

'Yes.'

'No, it'll be fine.'

'Suit yourself.'

Hilary was having fun. She wanted it gift-wrapped. She was starting to look around the place, her eyes agog.

I paid and we made our escape. At the door, however, I remembered and had to return to ask for a receipt. The transaction seemed to take forever. I guess not too many customers asked for receipts. Eventually we made it outside to the fresh air. Neither of us wanted to hold the box. We juggled it between us. Out on the footpath we yielded to our hysteria and laughed till our eyes watered, our voices quite shrill. No one took any notice of us. We blended right in with life on Darlinghurst Road.

'Let's have a look at it,' said Hilary.

'We can't.'

'Sure we can.'

I carefully opened the box and we peered in—there was a flash of flesh colour—but it was too awful to contemplate, so I slammed the lid shut. We laughed some more, weeping, recalling what we had seen inside the Venus Love-In.

'Right up his bottom . . . ' Hilary squealed.

Exhausted and drained, we wandered arm in arm down the road with the penis pump we had bought for a stranger under my elbow. A good deed, you'd have to think of it as a good deed, of all the good deeds possible, life going on all around us, chaotic, rambling, vaguely familiar.

Bluey and Myrtle

'Who's a pretty boy then?'
'Who's a pretty boy then?'
'Give us a kiss.'
'Give us a kiss.'
'Who's a pretty boy?'

I'm the pretty boy. No one else. Pretty Bluey. Me. My pretty plumage.

'Who loves his Mummy then?'
'Who loves his Mummy then?'
'Who's been making a great big mess?'

That's going too far. Yes, I repudiate that. Pretty is as pretty does.

Three thousand six hundred and fifty-three days, but who's counting? I'm getting on. Each morning like this one, the same beginning. The same light bulb burning brightly in the ceiling. How have we come to this?

Myrtle.

Myrtle's eyes vast and rheumy behind her glasses. She places a sunflower seed between her lips and presses her face up against the wires of the cage. Her lips make a plastic smooching noise, pursed around the seed like an anus. Pretty Bluey knows all about simile and metaphor. I used to read the newspapers spread out on the table below, over the shoulder of the old fellow. He was a great one for the crosswords. She expects me to bounce on my perch, bob my head, and take the seed from between her lips. I do. It's a kind of frigid, bestial kiss.

This is morning.

She scratches the cere of my beak with a fingernail. I hold the seed in my claw and examine it. I crack it open and nibble the kernel. Stale. What does she expect, a thank you?

'Give us a kiss,' she says.

'Give us a kiss,' I reply.

It doesn't matter how I say the words, I don't have to mean them. It's echolalia. She fills my seed tray and water bowl too. The same water bowl, all these years. Her giant hand squeezing in through the tiny gate. I grip the dowel rod of the perch as the cage rocks. My mirror and bell swing wildly on their chain, creating the illusion of cheerful, if fragmented company. Ha! When once it swung on its umbilicus of string, Twitters, my mate, was so offended by its patronizing attempt to create a society for us that he pecked through the thread and let it fall. Myrtle hooked it back up with an old watch chain, so now it twirls forever of its own accord, swinging in the breeze, reflecting a spasm of sunlight. Unless it was the old fellow who hooked it back up. It was his watch.

'Doesn't Bluey like his breakfast?' Myrtle says.

I deign to reply. For God's sake Myrtle put the cover back on. It's torture. I squawk rudely. The bouncing sun dazzles my eyes at random moments. She doesn't understand. She thinks it affectionate play when I peck at the little mirror, when in reality I am trying to rip my own impostor's eyes out. Each morning, when the cover is removed, the sudden galaxy of the kitchen is a shock to my delicate system. It's too big. Too noisy, when she bangs about in the cupboards after the sinister peace of the night. I'm all on edge when she clatters amongst the saucepans looking for something she cannot find, muttering, muttering.

Myrtle, put the cover back on; go back to bed; put us both out of our misery.

At dusk she comes to arrange the frilly curtain (she made it herself) over the dome of my cage. It's hardly an aviary, although when Twitters was alive, yes, yes, this perch thy centre was, these bars thy spheare. We'd splash in the dish and flap water out onto the crosswords below. No happier pair of lovebirds could you find, discussing all the issues of the day. (Oh Twitters.) She used to let us out, one at a time, to flutter about the wide open skies of the kitchen. Perch on the curtain rods. Or else on her finger. Once Twitters banged into the window pane. Lord how I squawked. We saw the mynah birds in their robbers' masks outside the window, bullying the sparrows. Ruling the roost. Noisy miscreants. In turn we flew ecstatic circles around the light shade. If only she had let us both out at once, escape might have been feasible. Once the old fellow came in unexpectedly. His snowy hair looked right for nesting material, but that was just instinct.

'Quickly Alf, shut the door.'

'Jesus, they're loose.'

'Only one is loose. I'm training them.'

'What for, combat?'

What a terrible glimpse of freedom that was; that chasm of possibility. Did Twitters contemplate it? For one to leave the other and cross the threshold. It was unthinkable. So we returned dutifully to our coop, wing muscles stiffening after exercise, glad, it must be said, to be home. Mandela's cell was much bigger when he lived in it.

Until one day—that tragic day—I woke to find the tiny heart of Twitters had given up the ghost and he had dropped off his perch. Diminished and flat in the sawdust at the bottom of the cage. I'll never forget poor Myrtle's face when she came to remove the cover and saw my love, cold and shrivelled on the floor; the rictus of his beak; his claws gripped as if around a seed. She nearly had a fit. *18 across, 10 letters: abolition of sudden diminution of sensation and voluntary motion*—what could that be? Pencil scratching at the temple—apoplectic. No other word for it. Poor duck. Like that too when she found the old fellow.

From that day on I took it on myself to rid the cage of every death-infected scrap of sawdust that she persists in shovelling into my habitat. My world. Not hers. With great diligence I scratch and flick them out between the bars at night. It has become part of the ritual. Dawn comes. The alarm rings. Her curtains rattle open. She hobbles downstairs with the pot. Empties it in the lav. Gives it a rinse. She fills the kettle. She gets the milk from the fridge. All these things I know, with the extra sensory perception of the blind, even before she whips the floral shroud off the cage. *Squawk!* The glaring, naked bulb. Or else the piercing, eastern sun.

'Who's a pretty boy then?'

Her great, nude irises, paling with age.

'Come on Bluey, who's a pretty boy then?'

I take my head from under my wing, make the reply; *whistle, squawk, chirrup.*

'Who's been making a great big mess then?'

'Great big mess.'

She fetches the dustpan and brush from beneath the sink and sweeps up the contaminated shavings. I must say that apart from my obsessive compulsion I rather like the look of the flakes as they float gently down through the moonlight. And the breast feathers I have torn out with my own beak and tossed overboard. I am the life-giving pelican drawing its own blood to feed its young. But there are no young. There is no one.

16 across, 4 letters: the focus of solipsism, — — — — sacrifice.

Cover off. Light on. Day begun. I watch Myrtle at her rituals. She takes the kettle off the stove and fills the teapot. Twirls it three times. The milk. The strainer. The careful pouring. The dreadful humanity of it. It took her a long time to learn she only needed one cup. *Chirp chirp chirp.* I'm here too. Without each other old girl, where are we?

'Who's a pretty boy then?' I try to encourage her, but she seems distracted this morning. Instead of putting the kettle back on the stove she puffs out the flame like a candle, puts the kettle on the table. The milk bottle goes in a cupboard. That look on her face, she's trying to remember something, like a word on the tip of her tongue. Someone's birthday. Whose can it be? I gaze down on her grey curls. Myrtle, Myrtle, (I want to shriek) let's set aside this grieving we've both grown so used to. The bald and bleeding patch on my breast throbs where I have dug out the roots of my quills. Something in my whistle alerts her. Despair perhaps. She comes to stare through the wire. The fading cerulean blue of her eyes. Sometimes, when the mirror spins, I understand that it is only me whom I glimpse in dizzy reflection; yet part of me could swear that I am not alone, and it is Twitters, my love, risen off the floor, returned to me. What a mystery, the apperception of consciousness.

Myrtle presses her lips to the bars. Her face is near.

'Who's a pretty boy?'

Squaaawk! Twitters. Twitters was the pretty boy. A downright flirt. I wonder if I have time to peck out an eye? No. She's fast for an old duck.

Her tea. Her breakfast. Her washing up. I can't go on, so I suppose I'll go on.

'Oh my goodness Bluey, you haven't had your muesli.'

I have Myrtle. I have. Look. Don't you remember? She'll forget me altogether one day. Just as she's forgotten to turn the gas off. Listen, hissing steadily from the ring. *Chirp.* Heroic deeds of Bluey the mining canary, asphyxiated in the patriotic line of duty. I could have told her you don't blow out the flame like a birthday candle. She calls the mishmash she gives me 'muesli'. The old fellow used to laugh at that. It was his job to mix the sesame and sunflower seeds in an empty jam tin, to lift the little gate with his great hairy fingers, as Myrtle does now, to slide the saucer of seed in through the aperture. She balks when she sees that my tray is already full.

'Oh dear,' she says, 'Aren't you hungry?'

No, I'm not hungry. The open gate is a guillotine, stoppered up by her hand. She takes out the still full dish and replaces it with another full dish.

'Now Bluey, what was I looking for? I suppose I'll remember when I find it.'

Myrtle turns back to the sink. The gate is open. Stuck at the top. All those hideous mynah birds in the branches outside the windows. There are more of them these days. Murderous fecundity. The kitchen is frightening enough. I could casually flop down from my perch, peck at the seed, as on any normal morning, give a spontaneous gargle of song, before tugging down on the gate, as Twitters used to do when Myrtle forgot to close it, so we were safe again. I call out, 'Myrtle, Myrtle, shut the gate.'

I could say anything, she wouldn't hear. She's busy doing the dishes. Humming. She's forgotten me. There's a whole day to get through. No one ever bothers to visit anymore. But there's something about this morning, something about the fundamental limitations of language as a means of communication between two sentient beings.

'Myrtle the turtle,' I squawk, 'You've left the gas on. *Poo-tee-weet!*'

I smell the gas rising. Thick and fast. It won't be long now Twitters. I suppose, like me, she has her own memories of the old fellow. The look on her face when she came in to find him on the kitchen floor beneath us, the new bulb in his hand, an

67

Osram from memory, the step ladder on its side. Sparks every-where. *18 across, 10 letters.* No muesli that day, I can tell you. Nor, a year later, when Twitters was removed in a tissue. In a tissue for God's sake! Cold as a frog. His legs pitifully thin compared to the rest of him. Christ only knows what happened after that. No, it's Myrtle and me. And she's left the gas on. And the trapdoor open. The stove hissing softly in the corner like a bronchial lung. Listen Myrtle I don't want to pine away up here forever, why don't you buy another pretty boy to keep me company; some handsome, androgynous *Melopsittacus undulatus*, with green tail feathers for preference. I'll teach him how to speak real proper like.

I hop down from my perch. Ruffle my wings. Scratch myself.

'Who's a pretty boy then?'

'Who's a pretty boy then?' she answers.

'I am Myrtle, I am.'

She doesn't skip a beat. Dish, fork, plate, knife, spoon, bowl.

'And who made a great big mess then?'

'I did Myrtle, I did.'

I nibble the seed. I stretch my otiose wings. They make a noise like flags on a windy day. Small flags, I admit, flapping in the winds of destiny. I see the open window beyond the open cage. The yellow masks of mynah birds in the trees outside. Myrtle is humming. A bee in her bonnet that she doesn't know is there. Dish, fork, plate, knife, spoon, bowl. She's washing the same cut-lery that she's washed already. I stand beneath the rusted door. I will it to drop, but it is not heavy and would probably only give me a clonk on the beak. Fate is beckoning, or is it opportunity? I take off.

Freedom. *Flap flap flap.*

'Oh Bluey, Bluey come back,' Myrtle squawks, dropping the dish mop.

I circumnavigate the airspace of the kitchen.

Cheep.

'Come back you naughty bird.'

I perch on the curtain rod. Morning ablution down the drapes.

'Oh Bluey.'

I buzz the kitchen. Strafe the dishes. The gas is thicker up near the ceiling. I'm a raptor! Bank away from the open window. The mynahs are watching the whole charade. Plenty of dust up here on the cupboards where she can't reach anymore. I soar. I glide. I loop the loop. My stunted wings clip the hot Osram in the socket of the ceiling. It must be loose for, surprisingly, it plummets to the floor. Newton's light bulb. I watch it plummet as if in slow motion. Down, down. Shatters on the lino with a soft pop, making Myrtle jump. Thin slivers of glass, like fish scales, scatter under the fridge and stove. The room darkens appreciatively. I swoop.

'Come back Bluey.'

'Not on your life. I'm free! *Poo-tee-weet.*'

What does she want? You give a chap language and then expect subservience? God did not decree that consciousness be solely of the human sphere. Anthropoavian, surely that's a crossword clue.

'Oh Bluey, what a mess.'

'You bet, sister.'

I swoop again. I chirp my heart out. I am faced with the open window or the empty cage. In or out. Zenith versus nadir. It's not often I really get to think about these paradoxes. About where

I belong. *Ask rather what the universe has done to deserve me?* Where the light bulb has fallen from the ceiling, the socket is open and exposed. The switch by the door is still on. As it was when the old fellow was still with us. He wouldn't listen when Twitters warned him to dry his hands first. Cause and effect. First law of electrical conductivity. I'm coming Twitters. The temptation is too great. I swoop. I soar. A phoenix risen from the sawdust. Blaze of glory. Sparks everywhere. Socket open. Up through the gas I rise on eagle's wings unto the flowering hypothesis of Heaven.

Leaving the Diggings

Chi So was burned in the Chinese oven in the cemetery where the smoke sent the choughs startling up into the air. Not so much his own smoke, but the incense and cymbals ringing and the keening of the mourners as they farewelled his soul off to the afterlife. The choughs whistled a warning arpeggio like a carillon in the trees. They sat on some low branches chortling over their hymnals and testaments at all this curious human activity. Ethel could not understand the prayers and devotions for Chi So, but the cymbals sounded nice and the sun was warm on the black lace of her shawl. Some of the men were crying. Ethel's mother, Mrs Mary Anderson, stood beside her and she could tell from the rigidity of her spine she was very angry.

'Listen,' Ethel whispered, although Mrs Anderson was not listening, as someone picked a few sad notes on a Chinese lute or mandolin, as if the reeds of a riverbank were playing an elegy.

After the funeral Ethel's mother lead her away saying, 'We have to find a way to get out of this place.'

Ethel used to think that choughs were cruel looking birds, bad omens like carrion crows, until she saw them scuffing through leaf mulch in the forest in a clumsy sort of way, like so many sailors with wooden legs. Apostle birds, as they are also known, are as diligent fossickers as a family of Chinese diggers sifting through a mullock heap. Both could find any old thing from a worm to a worn out boot to a freckle of gold overlooked by your unobservant local prospector. Unfortunately, the mullock heap Chi So had been turning over had not been irrevocably abandoned by its owner, a man called Hamish Tunks. Tunks, who, returning unexpectedly, had found Chi So 'jumping his claim', as he announced and, exercising summary justice, given him a hiding with a pick handle.

Mrs So brought her injured husband to the Post Office where Mary Anderson lived with Ethel. She was extremely upset. Ethel's father had been a doctor but by that stage he was dead, and her mother, being the wife of a doctor, could not help, even though people expected her to, especially women having babies. However, she did take them to the hospital up the road, pushing him in a wheelbarrow, but he was bleeding from the ear and there was a haemorrhage in his brain bag and after about ten days he did not wake up again.

As Postmistress, Mrs Anderson was about the only person acting in any official capacity that the town had. The good-for-nothing troopers did not count. They were what made her so angry in the first place. All they did was put Hamish Tunks in the police cell until he sobered up, then gave him what amounted to a stern talking to; a dressing down with some harsh words. Mrs Anderson refused to serve Hamish Tunks after that, a token protest because Tunks could neither write nor read any letters he may have received, which he did not. In the street, if they met, Mrs Anderson called him a 'drunken sot', which only made him laugh. Others did not share her opinion in favouring the Chinese.

It was Ethel's job to deliver mail that had not been collected in a good while, that is, if they knew the miners were still in the district. Because the Chinese miners never knew when their mail had arrived, their camp was a place she sometimes ran to, maybe once or twice a month. As soon as she stepped off the boardwalk outside the Warnock Bros store she would hoist up her pinny and tear down the Castlemaine road to the Chinese camp by Sandy Creek.

'Don't stay there too long,' her mother's warning voice chided in her ears, though what she was warning against was not clear to her daughter.

After a day stuck inside the schoolhouse there was nothing she liked better than a good tear. She could imagine she was on a horse galloping far away. On a scorcher she would take off her shoes and stockings and stand in the creek water and wriggle her toes in the sand. In the Chinese camp, secreted within the Chinaman's bush, she would give the mail to Mrs So, who would later distribute it amongst the fifteen or twenty Chinamen living there. They were always out digging when Ethel brought the mail, but she noted evidence of their habitation—mah-jong tiles piled up waiting for the evening game; various instruments she did not know the names of; cooking pots; laundry. Mrs So would take the mail with a nod, then wave the girl away to the freedom of the afternoon.

On the day of Chi So's funeral, Mary Anderson locked the door of the Post Office, unheard of on a Tuesday, and stepped out in her best dress. Striding purposefully, she took Ethel to join the *cortege* winding along the Maryborough Road. The borrowed cart bearing Chi So's knocked-together coffin had a buckled axle and seemed to roll along with a squeaky limp. They stood at the rear of the assembly about the Chinese oven in the Maldon cemetery. Choughs warbling in the trees. They were the only white people there. Mrs Anderson's lips were stern and thin. She wanted nothing more than to be away from that terrible, beautiful place, and away from that terrible town.

'Listen,' whispered Ethel, 'What's that sound?'

'Cymbals.'

'What do they mean?'

'I don't know. Death.'

Mrs Anderson had liked Chi So and also Mrs So who was always polite and let Ethel touch her silken bonnet. Silk was hard to come by on the gold fields. It was a little treasure. The post-mistress used to say, 'Well if it isn't Mr and Mrs So and So.'

But they did not get her private joke. Mrs So would plop her letters on the counter with their strange inscriptions spidering over the envelopes. Ethel guessed they were sending news, and maybe even money back to their people in China. Ethel's mother often allowed her to lick the stamps and thump them onto the corner of the envelopes with her fist. It made a nice, solid noise on the bench top. Mrs So also accompanied the other Chinese miners when they came to post their letters, perhaps because her English was a little better, even though her English was precious poor. She smiled a lot, making use of her fingers. Mrs Anderson seemed to understand that language. One day Mrs So brought in an abacus and they had a high old time discussing the workings of that instrument in words neither of them exactly shared.

The men never spoke.

If Ethel licked too many stamps she would get a queasy feeling in her stomach and have to go find a dunny can.

Ethel was the only girl in Maldon, apart from her mother, who could play the piano. The trouble they had in freighting such an object up to the diggings at that time was not a thing to be dismissed lightly. It was an Albrecht upright and it looked a peculiar sight, like a gryphon, on the back of the dray, which brought it from Bendigo, groaning a painful chord at every bump in the road. It took four men to lower it safely down and carry it inside, and boy did they huff and puff about it. Although she never said anything Ethel knew her mother was upset at the cost. So Ethel took her lessons and practised every day because she was grateful, she truly was. Music was all she had since her father passed away.

'How well do you remember your father?' Mrs Anderson sometimes asked.

It was a conversation Ethel always found awkward because she remembered him vividly, his smell and his prickles, things that upset her to recall. Yet her mother seemed to think these memories were not worthy of him, that her own memories were somehow the proper sort.

Sometimes they played a duet, or a cantilena sitting side by side in the evening light. There used to be an old miner from Galway who came in specially to ask Mrs Anderson if he could have a tinkle. He was so out of practice and his fingers so rusted with spade work he could only get a little *diddley-dee* music out of it. It was Ethel's father's sort of music, jigs and reels. Mrs Anderson saw that it made him teary to think of his old home. So she made a rule, 'We shall have no music in this house but that we make ourselves,' she said.

One day after Mr and Mrs So and So had finished their business with her mother, Ethel glimpsed them through the window where she was practising her Chopin. They were simply standing on the street looking at the gutters which people had put more effort into building than their own homes. She supposed they were taking a moment to enjoy the sunshine. Ethel stretched her hands to the octaves, but they did not quite reach. A couple of the cushions had gone, or come loose on two keys so there was only a clunky wooden sound in one, and a buzz coming from another which made her ears wince. They were saving up to have them repaired. In the meantime Ethel would have to imagine those notes and grit her teeth. In a way they made her understand Chopin's notes even more individually. She was hoping the piano tuner would come one day soon to work his magic.

'But why can't he come?'

'Because we can't afford him.'

'I don't see the point, Mother, of buying a piano and then not being able to play it properly.'

'If we went to Melbourne we'd be able to hear a real piano, but we can't afford that either.'

'You make it sound like we're trapped here by my piano.'

'Maybe Ethel, maybe we shall need to sell it.'

Ethel was aghast. 'Whoever would buy it here?'

Ethel glanced up from her score. She had moved on to an Air from the Watermusic by then, and noticed, not the inquisitive face of Chi So at the window, but rather his flattened ear at the glass. She was able to examine the squashed and hairy ear of the Chinaman for some moments until he realised she had stopped playing. When he saw she had spotted him, he touched his funny hat, gave a little bow, and scurried away.

On Sundays when the Post Office and the Penny School were closed Mrs Anderson allowed her daughter to climb to the top of Mt. Tarrengower where there was an impressive view, and where a breath of clean air might be had. There was no danger from the blacks because they mostly hated Mt. Tarrengower and called it 'Leanganook' which Ethel thought a beautiful word except that it meant the 'ugly lump' or some such. In German it is *garstig*. She liked the story of one curious native, watching a miner rinsing his pan at a cradle, who guffawed at the foolish fellow spending all that energy washing his stones, only to throw them away again. She supposed there was comedy in talking at cross purposes, but wondered if that was all? If miscomprehension had its own agenda. Everyone had a different word for things; the Blacks, the Chinese, the Indians, the Germans. She liked to hear the tumbling music of new words. *Wassermusik*, for one; *gryphon*, for another.

In any event the mountain still had plenty of miners crawling all over it. In the years before the Anderson's arrived, when gold fever had been an epidemic, there had been more. You could tell how populated the place had been by the rubbish left behind. However, there were still loads of eager fellows to keep the febrile feeling of gold in the air, as if the world was a jolly old square dance and the water was champagne. Most of them knew the Postmistress's daughter. Some of them called out her name, even though she would have preferred to keep her name a secret.

'Good day, Miss Ethel.'

'Sing us a song, Miss Ethel.'

'Have you a stamp for me, Ethel?'

'Yes,' she cried to this last, 'put out your foot and I'll give you one.'

It was an old Post Office joke, but she meant it.

It wasn't Sunday, it was a Tuesday and she would not sing them a song. She did not want to talk to them. She had to get to the top of the mountain. There were tents scattered higgledy-piggledy all over the side of the hill amongst the tree stumps and yellow gorse. New saplings budding back where the older trees had been chopped down. Many of the miners were up to their necks in mullock holes, shovelling up spadefuls of scree and clay and general rubble. The exposed bones of quartz scattered about like a stone ossuary.

In days gone by if she had had the bad luck to fall into a mullock hole it would be a soft landing because there would have been a miner in every one. A miner dazzled with a dream of lighting his pipe with a five pound note. Many had moved on. Those who remained had invested much sweat in their mullock hole, it was hard for them to give it up. Ethel didn't know how they made their selection: the set of the rocks in the ground a lucky sign perhaps, the vision of riches beckoning. For others, dreams faded soon enough. As such there were a lot of deserted shafts, which made the place precarious. Everywhere smelled of freshly turned earth.

Panting, she climbed on. It was about three miles to the top of the hill. From various vantage points she could gaze in awe down the barren hillside. The township of Maldon lay at the foot of the mountain, its busy main streets shaped like a tired Y lying on its side; the High street lined with carts and drays. The tracks winding off to Bendigo and Castlemaine like ribbons lost in the grass. Streamers of smoke rose up from camping fires spread throughout the scrub. Smoke especially from the Government Gold Battery and the Beehive chimney where the big companies continued to process their ore. To the south beyond Oswald's mine and Carmen's tunnel stood the remains of extinct volcanoes.

There had been upward of twenty thousand miners turning over the ground in the Maldon vicinity. And the ground was ravaged. There was not a flower. You couldn't even hear a bird sing. The smoke from the cyanide vats and quartz kilns fell on the town;

the roaring cacophony from the stamper batteries and crushing machines—all Ethel could see was bedlam. The calx lying about the kilns like roasted knuckles. It was like something Milton had dreamed up to entertain Satan. Yet gradually the noise faded the higher up the mountain Ethel climbed. Over the north of the town the nearby Nuggety Ranges, like a section of the earth's disinterred vertebrae. The plains stretched away in every direction, seeming to promise so much, yet failing comprehensively to deliver it. Everything seemed determined to drive the music out of the girl because, from the top of the hill, there was nowhere else to go but back down.

Sometimes she felt as though the only civilized thing on all the diggings, like a cornered creature with yellow teeth, was her piano. Standing there, sweating in the breeze, on the day of Chi So's funeral she put her face in her hands and, because she felt she was too young to scream, she wept.

About ten or twelve days afterwards a parcel of letters arrived with the strange and beautiful Chinese writing on them. Someone had tried their hand at translating into English because one of the letters was addressed to *So, Chi, Maldon P.O. Victory.* Her mother, writing some letters of her own, said she must take the mail to the Chinese camp at once.

'Why must I?'

'Because it is your duty. And because I am exhausted,' said Mrs Anderson, who had let the mask of her official position fall away and sat slumped in a chair. Often the only time she seemed happy was when she had a tea cup in hand.

The Chinese miners made their camp by Sandy Creek in the thickets of Chinaman's bush where you wouldn't even tether a sheep so fine and irritating were the seeds. Ethel wasn't sure if 'thicket' was the right word. Nor jungle. Not many of the Chinese had brought their wives, so Chi So must have been a leader amongst them. His letter felt heavy in her hand. Ethel thought about him being buried so far from his own home with nothing to remember him by but a Chinese brick oven.

Along the way various miners poked their heads up like rabbits out of their holes.

'Good day, Miss Ethel.'

'Any letters for me, Miss Ethel?'

A face appeared at the lip of the earth. It was Hamish Tunks grinning at her.

'Hello girly,' he said.

She made no reply. There was the taste of glue in her mouth as she hurried on.

A little commune of tents and lean-to's lay sheltered within the copse of Chinaman's bush. 'Copse' was not the right word either. One day, Ethel thought, she would find the right word. One day she would also find the right word for 'brain bag.' A protective ring of stones contained the charcoal of a cooking fire. She could see no evidence of people in the camp, just the cooking pots and mah-jong tiles. Ethel called out 'Mrs So', but there was no response. Too frightened to barge in through the thicket she dawdled there a while then, feeling silly, turned back with the letters towards home. She could come back tomorrow. Chi So would not miss his mail. However she did not want to return the way she had come, because of Tunks. She kept her eyes on the ground hoping she would not stub her toe on a nugget, as some of the tall tales would have you believe. She would not have wanted to be turned into one of them, a fevered, gold-struck, jiggering fool living in a hole in the ground like a bandicoot.

Near the creek at the back of D'Orsa's cottage towards the Castlemaine road, Ethel heard a note of strange music. She knew it was not a bird, although they could be musical if you found the right one, but a type of music she had only recently heard. She paused. There was another. She went towards the sound, peering through some stubborn bushes. In a moment Ethel came across the figure of Mrs So in her silk bonnet, sitting by a water hole where some prospector had excavated beneath the tree roots. The instrument she played was not unlike a lute, or pictures Ethel had seen of a lute in one in her father's books. However the music was quite different, single notes, not chords, plucked from the four or five strings. In a while Mrs So stopped playing and the silence was replaced by the sudden screech of a cockatoo sounding like a sheet being ripped in a gale. The bird flapped off, and then there was just the wind itself, softly in the trees. Then quiet.

Suddenly, in fright, Mrs So turned and saw Ethel. She breathed, and studied the girl through her reddened, swollen eyes, turning back to the creek in which she seemed to be pouring the lonely music of her grief. She began to play again. Ethel didn't know how long she stood there, but without being fully aware of it she found she had drawn closer. She stood by Mrs So's side and watched her pluck those new notes. Then Mrs So looked up and, like something weary and raw, gestured for Ethel to sit.

She did so. A stone dug into her thigh. After a while she pointed at the instrument the woman held and asked, 'What is this called?'

The woman shrugged, leaving her shoulders up for quite a while, then said: 'Pipa.'

'Pipa?'

Ethel tested the word. Mrs So offered it and Ethel, in turn, handed her the parcel of letters, uppermost being the letter addressed to *So, Chi, Maldon P.O. Victory.*

The instrument, the pipa, was pear shaped, its smooth back round against Ethel's stomach. She examined it closely while Mrs So, reluctantly it seemed, opened the first letter. A happy letter, with lots of news, from someone who did not yet know that the person addressed would never read it. Ethel had watched the woman's fingers at the frets and so could guess at the chromatic scale. She tried a string. She could not look at her face, though she was painfully aware of the woman reading at her side. Mrs So sniffed up some tears. Ethel took another note from it. Then another. The notes hovered in the air like birds suspended in flight. She played a short scale, a small tune, one note corresponding to the next, but the sound of it was too odd, too alien, and when Mrs So had finished reading the letter with its strange vertical columns she handed the pipa back.

They did nothing then, but stare at the water. Soon Mrs So rose to her feet and took the letters and her instrument and, as if blindly, turned towards her camp. Ethel stood also. In the distance the bald protuberance of Mt. Tarrengower, that ugly lump, *garstig,* rose to interrupt the sky. Ethel picked up a piece of quartz and threw it in the creek. *Wassermusik.*

She left the creek and went home; however the noise from the stamper batteries would not let her formulate her thoughts. She dearly wanted to be melancholy, but the noise of the machinery would not allow her to be anything.

She never told her mother about the pipa. Only that she had delivered the letters safely. Mrs Anderson had her own concerns.

After dinner Ethel buried her nose in her sheet music while her mother wrote another letter to the director of the asylum at Ararat where they had taken her husband to die and where his possessions still wanted collecting. Ethel could hear the pen scratching from across the room. She wondered what would now become of Mrs So in her silken bonnet, in a land whose language she could barely speak, a widow in a camp of twenty men without wives, their leader now dead. She could not imagine that situation, though maybe one day she might. Perhaps, she hoped, Mrs So had saved enough money now to leave the diggings and go home.

She tried to imitate the notes she had plucked from the pipa, but the harmony of it was not the same. Her fingers fell quiet at the keyboard. After a while her mother looked up from her stilled page; the lamp light unflickering.

'What's wrong Ethel?'

'I feel sad for Mrs So,' she said.

'Yes. I know what you mean.'

'I hope she can leave the diggings soon.'

'Oh dear child, so do I.'

Yet in their hearts they rued the day when they might have to witness Mrs So leaving on a cart, her belongings in a bag at her feet, and they, the surviving Andersons, remaining.

Political Correctness

Our ferry, the Lady Lipsom, skimmed across the glittering surface of the water like a stone skipping over a placid lake. Gulls hovered above us, as if on strings, squawking with menace. Apart from the queasiness I was rather enjoying myself, sitting out on the deck like the Queen of Sheba. Sea spray flicked up in the air occasionally, which was a relief. You could feel the heat of the sun like a bully standing over you. Dean, my husband, was asking one of the crew how many horsepower were under the hood. The ferryman, who had ropes to coil, looked annoyed at being distracted from his work. I was drowsy. The sunshine was soporific so that I couldn't even be bothered telling Dean to stop it. There was never any stopping him anyway. At one point, skating between small postcard islands in the sparkling sea, Dean nudged me in the ribs and nodded towards one of the other passengers. All I saw was a girl, brown as a berry, just about falling out of her top, and a man I did not recognise. I didn't know what Dean was on about, so I closed my eyes again. It was a treat to do nothing. The bright inside of my eyelids the jewelled, ruby colour of all my troubles fading away.

They welcomed us at the dock with little plastic flutes of champagne. A nice touch, I reckoned, all part of the deluxe service we could expect. Some of the passengers received *leis*, although we didn't. Dean found a trolley for our bags and wheeled it up the path. Our room was on the second floor and there was a tiny little elevator so we wouldn't have to be bothered with the stairs.

'Not so squeezy, eh?' Dean said, making some lame joke. We were already in each other's personal space.

We settled in. The resort was just as glossy as the brochures had promised. I emptied my leopard skin patterned suitcase (fake), bought from a touter at Circular Quay, onto the bed and fossicked through the contents for my togs. I was going to hit the pool. Daydream Island, the place second honeymoons were made of. Wedding anniversaries too, I hoped. The bed was nice and firm. Plenty of free shampoo and tea bags. The tropical prints on the walls reminding you, in case you had forgotten, of paradise.

Outside it was beautiful as a movie set. I couldn't believe it. It sure beat the Rooty Hill RSL. We had the pool all to ourselves, despite the bikinis and beautiful bods all over the place. The sun glared off the water as I took a quick dunk. It felt like the world was at my beck and call, I only had to snap my fingers. I ordered a drink which came with a little paper umbrella in it. The waiter brought it out to me on my banana lounge. Dean was fidgeting beside me on his own banana lounge. There was nothing for him to tinker with.

'How do you like that?' he said, eventually.

'What?'

'These bastard politicians ruining our holiday.'

Dean was wearing his new Hawaiian shirt open at the neck, and down below, his Speedos tucking his bundle into a tight little knot beneath the full moon of his stomach. I wondered if he would consider walking down Pitt St. like that? He looked ridiculous but I wasn't going to be the one to tell him. Let him work it out for himself. For a second he eclipsed the sun.

'Who's ruining your holiday, Dean?'

I was keen to return to the doorstopper I had bought at the airport. I hadn't even got past all the waffle yet. I had claimed my place by the pool, under a palm tree, I had my fancy drink and I was not budging.

'Sinclair, or Brereton, one of those crusty politicians. I don't know which one. That bloke who was always on the news, the Minister for something.'

'What about him?'

'He's here. I saw him on the ferry. With some girl. And just now I saw them walking down to the beach. He's got legs like toothpicks. Doesn't he know how silly he looks?'

'Did you say hello?'

'No fear. I hate the bastards. Freeloaders. Here at the taxpayer's expense.'

'Did I vote for him?'

'I don't know Shona. You never tell me who you vote for.'

I thought about that little secret and the mischievous power it gave me.

'Don't politicians deserve a holiday like everyone else?'

'He's retired. Got booted out of office. Lurks and perks for the rest of his life.'

I could see Dean was annoyed, but I wasn't going to let it light my gander. He often did silly things when he got worked up over nothing, and I was here for a rest.

Daydream Island. Playground of the Whitsunday archipelago. I had done my research. It had been Dean's dream for six years to bring me here. He'd seen something about it on one of the travel shows. He had accrued some long service leave, as well as some stress leave, and I had taken some leave without pay. Along with superannuation, long service leave was one of Dean's favourite topics of conversation. I often told him to get over it, he could get run down by a bus tomorrow. He said that was just wishful thinking. He's been under a bit of strain. I would just as soon have stayed home and gone to the club with the girls, but Dean had his heart set on it, so I collected a few brochures from the travel agent and began to come around to the idea. Everyone in the photos looked so tanned and buffed. The drinks so comical. I would save the little umbrellas to show the girls back on the Ward.

I must say that Daydream Island appeared to be the perfect choice. It was a paradise. All those palm trees. Not too far from the mainland. All that squeaky sand. And the water so beautiful, crystal clear—what do they call it?—turquoise—and warm, like a fresh bath.

'He doesn't have a job,' Dean continued, 'He lost the last election, or maybe it was the one before that.'

'I didn't vote for him.'

I could see that my doorstopper would have to wait.

A funny blue fly landed on my cossie and began sucking the chlorine from it.

'Yet what's he doing here?' Dean asked rhetorically. He was like a dog with a bone.

'I tell you it's a disgrace.'

'You tell him, Dean.'

'Don't worry, I will. I spoke to the barman, and do you know what he said?'

'I guess I don't.'

'He told me that Brereton, or Sinclair, whichever one it is, has been here twice a year for the last five years.'

'Lucky him.'

'At the taxpayer's expense!'

'You said that.'

'I mean Shona, that *we're* paying for it. Indirectly, but still, it pops my clog.'

I flicked back a page in my book, trying to make a point. I'd already forgotten what was going on. So far it bore no resemblance to the blurb on the back cover, or the title. The fly took off for greener pastures and Dean flapped his hand at it. I could feel the sun burning me already, so I made free with the factor thirty plus.

'And what did he ever give you, Dean?'

'Nothing. That's what. A big fat nothing. I'm gonna have words to him.'

'Don't do anything rash. Remember you're here to relax.'

I took a sip from my drink. Mmm.

'Rash! Rash? I'll give him rash. It kind of takes the chill off your champers, knowing he's kicking back, not paying for it. I'll empty the bar fridge and charge it to his tab, that's what I'll do. Your shout Sinkers, ha!'

'Shh . . . You'll probably empty the bar fridge anyway.'

'I'm gonna give him a piece of my mind.'

'Only a small piece, I hope.'

Dean brandished his fist. 'I'm gonna give him a *vox pop* right on the end of his chin.'

'Calm down. Do you want some of this?' I asked, holding out the sun block, but he shook his head.

A lonely little daisy was growing in a crack in the concrete by the edge of the pool. Imagine, surviving all that treated water, and in this heat. Nature was wonderful. I got to my feet and moved the banana lounge into the shade. It was the most exercise I had done all morning. Then I flopped back into the water. The bubbles roared in my ears. At last Dean shut up, but only for a moment because when I surfaced he was still going hammer and tongs, saying he was fed up to his eye teeth, saying he was going to walk to the point. Good.

The sun was high and I thought it was important to stay out of the midday glare. You could see why these tropical luxury resorts plug *shade* as one of their most popular attractions. They had shade cloths hanging all over the outdoor areas. A young waiter brought me another drink and hung about nattering, paying me attention, telling me I should walk to the point if I get a chance.

Most people, I have deduced, talk too much, and I include myself in this sweeping generalization.

When Dean came back from the point a couple of hours later he was sunstruck and frazzled. He'd forgotten his hat. I saw that he hadn't yet walked the steam out of his system. He reported that he'd seen Sinkers (or Brereton) snorkelling in the shallows with a woman young enough to be his daughter.

'Perhaps she was his daughter Dean.'

'That's just what he wants us to think.'

'Well, there's nothing wrong with snorkelling.'

'That's only your opinion.'

I had to piece this together, just like the exposition in my weighty book, because, as they say in the classics, my husband was dazed and confused. I thought a walk would have done him some good, but clearly not. He was hot to the touch. He drank a lot of water. And then he drank a lot of beer.

In his words Dean had glared at the couple before continuing on to the point. When he reached it he saw it wasn't actually pointy. More of a bump. A corner. He climbed a small sand hill. He saw a little crab with one lemon claw struggling up the slope. The sea all around. There were some nice rocks. Periwinkles. He had a dip and within minutes his shirt was dry again. Then he turned around and, like Robinson Crusoe, retraced his own footsteps along the beach. By the time he reached the snorkelling spot the politician, if indeed he was a politician—('A sponge on human society is what he is')—had left the tepid water and was reclining with his lady friend in the manner of holidaymakers beyond the scrutiny of the public eye. To be precise they were reclining—

'In the nuddy if you please!'

Again Dean had looked daggers at them.

'Rubbing bloody coconut oil into her back. Hiding behind an umbrella. Would any decent father be doing that?'

'Perhaps she's not his daughter, Dean?'

'You said she was his daughter.'

'How would I know? It's a wonder she didn't cook in this heat.'

'This is what I've been telling you, Shona. Power corrupts.'

Dean had a slightly delirious look in his eyes. His feet looked sore and angry.

His scalp pink as a hot saucepan. Luckily he had kept his shirt on.

After doctoring him in our room we ate in the restaurant, *a la carte*. Dean resented that the politician was served before us. Afterwards he fell asleep, and I watched some telly. The weather map was so different from the one I was used to.

The next morning he had a migraine and stayed in bed. Not me. All that tropical fruit for breakfast. A sign in the bathroom gave me the option of simply tossing my towel on the floor, which I thought was pandering a bit. They supplied racks. Some poor chambermaid would only have to pick it up. There was a concrete island in the middle of the pool where you could lie around pretending to be a seal with a martini. I got past the exposition and well into the plot, although my wet thumbs dampened the pages a bit.

When Dean emerged from our suite he looked pained and sheepish. He kept taking ice cubes out of the champagne buckets and melting them on his scalp. When he did not find much sympathy in my quarter he moped off. Where he went I did not know—back to the point for all I cared—but it was during this moping that he discovered, through some surreptitious detective work, that Brereton (or Sinkers) was staying in Cabin 17B, a comfy little bungalow with a mock palm frond roof overlooking the beach. Information he would store up and put to his advantage at a time of his own choosing. He spent the afternoon staying out of the sun, sucking mango pips.

After dinner again he disappeared. I ploughed on through my holiday reading. I loved hearing the sound of waves from our window, like tyres swishing on a wet road after a hot day. It was quite hypnotic. When Dean returned he told me he had sneaked down to Cabin 17B and saw the lights on. He seemed to think this was incriminating.

'Listening to opera, they were,' he spat.

'I hope you didn't do anything silly, Dean.'

'No I didn't. But I reserve the right to.'

'Don't talk rubbish.'

'I pay my taxes.'

'Dean, what if it's not him? What if it's only someone who looks like him?'

'Then he must be used to it.'

Sunburned or not my husband was becoming preoccupied with the politician. The Queensland sun had cooked his commonsense like an egg. His legs were crimson and he kept scratching at them. He went out of his way to keep an eye on the couple in order, he said, so as to avoid them. He wanted to prove he was having a better holiday. I did not really think that the politician would care all that much. His constituency had no doubt forgotten all about him. A parliamentary pension was the price of us never having to look at his ugly mug on the telly again or, more importantly, listen to his opinions. He was here with his young floozy having the time of his middle-aged retirement. And Dean was here with me.

That night he tried to rub coconut oil into my shoulders, but I told him to buzz off, I wanted to finish my chapter. All I needed was a little peace and quiet and someone else to do the dishes for a change. He hopped off the bed and opened the bar fridge, which had magically replenished itself. I rang the kids back home and it sounded like there was a party going on. So I didn't ring again. Whatever mess there was I would deal with when I got back. The next day I was booked to have a massage and a pedicure. I didn't care about anything else.

My plan was going smoothly. I didn't see Dean until after lunch when he suddenly appeared poolside to tell me what he'd done with his morning. It took only a moment to apprehend that his tone was of a rambling nature. (There, that's the influence too much holiday reading can have). After strolling to the point, he decided to go water skiing, he who had never been water skiing in his life. More sun. No hat.

'Why?'

'Because there was only one place left and I had to beat Brereton to it. I saw over his shoulder he was looking at the itinerary on the notice board. Something like that would be wasted on someone like him.'

'Did you have fun?'

'No. The water shoots straight up your quoit and now I've got sore feet and a sore ring.'

'Too much information, Dean.'

'It was like a douche with a fire hose. But at least I beat Brereton.'

'I'm sure there's a first aid box here, maybe they've got some Calendula cream.'

'Leave off,' Dean wheedled, embarrassed, as he hobbled off to the bathroom where I later found him cooling his feet in a tub of cold water.

While he was resting that afternoon I walked to the point myself to see what all the fuss was about. I saw a little crab with a lemon coloured claw. There were some nice rocks. The sea all around. I circumnavigated the entire island, but it wasn't very big. I was back at the pool before I knew it.

Even though I only had a choice of two outfits, what to wear that night for dinner was a serious problem. Our anniversary shindig. In the Tropical Paradise Bistro we noticed the politician and his mistress sitting in a shadowy booth drinking cocktails. They giggled and stroked each other. A fan chugged in the ceiling creating a warm draught that made the tablecloths flutter. Dean's nose was peeling. His cheeks looked rouged. He scratched his thighs. At one point he said, 'How do you spell cactus?'

'Why do you want to know?'

'I forget.'

His eyes were wide and bloodshot. He had dispensed with his shoes. He was positively addled.

'There he is. Look at him. No, don't look. Drinking it up at our expense.'

'Don't get worked up, Dean. He's just trying to enjoy himself, same as us.'

'I wonder if we're paying for his meal as well?'

'What do you mean "we"?'

'I mean "we", the Australian taxpayer.'

There was a candle between us. Dean blew it out because it was too hot.

'Their suitcases are brand new. Calfskin. Courtesy of the department of lurks and perks.'

'How do you know about their suitcases?'

'Never you mind how I know.'

'What did you do?'

'Nothing. I'm on holiday.'

'You did something.'

'What would I do?'

'Something silly.'

He stirred his beer with a spoon, but he couldn't keep it to himself.

'I broke in there. They have a bigger fridge than us. She has a diaphragm.'

'What? You broke into their bungalow?'

'It's not as though it was locked.'

'Please tell me you didn't take anything?'

'I was looking for their passports.'

'What on earth for? You don't need a passport. We're still in Australia.'

'That explains why I couldn't find them.'

'Oh my God, did you take anything?'

He shrugged. Our voices were tight little whispers. There was wax on the tablecloth. He picked at it with a fingernail.

'I don't believe this. How do you know she has a diaphragm? Did you look through their things?'

'No, you don't believe me. You have never believed me to be a man of my word—'

'Jesus.'

'Or a man of action.'

'Oh Dean, look how you're hobbling around after that water skiing stunt.'

'I'm gonna tell him that I've had it up to here'—saluting his sunburned forehead—'with supporting the lavish lifestyles of him and his mistresses. What did he ever do for us when he was in office?'

'Wasn't it something about the roads?'

'He gave us nothing. I'm gonna tell him—I'm gonna tell him that it's his shout for once.'

'Don't work yourself into a tizzy.'

But Dean had already done so, and I saw that in a rather manic way he was enjoying himself. I think he must have been a little concussed. After the entrée (oysters) and the main (lobster) Dean, much to my humiliation, pushed back his chair and rose.

'Where are you going?'

He did not answer.

'Sit down.'

He did not sit down.

'Come back.'

He did not come back. I could have walked out, but it was like watching a car crash in slow motion. He marched, or rather hobbled, over to the politician's table. His bare feet almost radiant in the candlelight. I hid behind a menu and peered over the top of it. Luckily I could not hear, but I saw my husband standing over them. He could be quite domineering sometimes, especially with bare, burned feet and his red, flaky nose. There were raised voices. I could not make out the words. I saw the politician pluck the napkin from his lap and slap it on the table. Other people in the restaurant were watching, including my young drink waiter. Eventually the politician seized Dean by the hand and shook it vigorously. I breathed a sigh of relief. Dean limped back to our table just as the dessert arrived. I lowered the menu and took a gulp of my wine.

'Well?'

'It's him. I knew it was.'

No damage done, it seemed.

'Did you give him a piece of your mind?'

'I certainly did.'

'And what did he give you?'

'He gave me his autograph.'

Dean showed me the signed napkin. The desserts were already melting in the agitated air. Dean took an ice cube and rubbed his scalp with it. It quickly melted and made him look as though he was sweating for other reasons.

'Are you all right, Dean?'

He looked at me strangely, his pupils dilated.

'What?'

'Are you all right?'

'No. No, I don't think I am.'

'I think you need to see a doctor.'

'Yes, I've been over-doing it.'

He stared at the small pool of his dessert. A singer was about to serenade us.

'Shona?'

He took something from his pocket and placed it on the table.

'Yes?'

'What am I gonna do with this diaphragm?'

Boy, Girl, View

Not enough time has been allowed to tell this story. Time is short and nothing worthwhile has yet emerged. It was going to be the story of a child who became a man and another child who became a woman, and how they were destined never to meet. Two stories in effect, converging to a single plot. Three stories if you allow for the history of the landscape, the encroaching symbol of the view.

Wait. The idea dawns that the story of the child who becomes a man already contains within it the dual narratives of both childhood and manhood. Two distinct ways of interacting with the world. Similarly the story of the child who becomes a woman. There—already five differing points of view, each its own tale to tell. Hang on. Is there not implied in each story of child as child both the progenitors and various caregivers of each respective infant? That is, girl and boy. Indeed yes. Then acknowledgement must be made at least of the father and mother of the boy, plus the father and mother of the girl. And each respective parent necessarily has their own history, their own childhoods to inform and distort the way that they live their lives. Still on page one we have in essence thirteen stories, that is if you include the view, each one demanding to be told. I can see already things are getting complicated. Perhaps, to simplify matters, we might allow that neither of the central protagonists, girl-woman, boy-man, is possessed or burdened by a father. That is quite within the bounds of credibility. Granted we may well lose some of the theatricality and dramatic tension of paternity, but we must cut our losses. Certainly there must have been a sperm, but the story of sperm is a rather simple, single-minded and repetitive one, and we are not talking parthenogenetically here. This is realism. All right, delete the fathers. That gets rid of four stories at one stroke. That is, father as child and father as father, multiplied by two, in both cases, to all intents and purposes—exposition. Assume rightly a sperm was involved.

Let us also assume the common tale of birth. Or for variety's sake perhaps we should imagine two different births. The girl's— easy, swift, with soft lighting, music, just enough discomfort to make it memorable. The boy's birth—premature, complicated, agonizing, as if to prepare for the tumultuous relationships he will later have to face. And to add a little spice let us pretend he is born in a haystack, inside a shed, while the family home burns across the yard in a cataclysmic scene designed to hold attention and evoke empathy. Not too improbable is it? Empathy? To simplify things further, let us have it that both mothers, as is not unheard of in the act of continuing the species, die, croak, pass on. No. That is labouring the point. The fledgling character of the mother of the girl who, it appears, is in the maternity ward of a hygienic city hospital, would doubtless have been revived by efficient hospital interns well versed in emergency procedures and indemnity insurance. In the hayshed, however, smoke of the nearby conflagration thickening the air, the eyes of the animals bright with alarm at the screaming, the scene is more involved. It is not hard to conjure the beads of sweat, the determination, the pain and blasphemy, the sudden silence. Soft miaow of the infant. The smell of blood on the straw. Let us embellish, perhaps anthropomorphically, the dumb pity and understanding of the animals: a horse, a goat, a cow. Imagine, please, the cow licking clean the newborn of his vernix, lowering her udder awkwardly to his lips. The searching, the latching on. Imagine also, because these things are seldom addressed in stories such as this is turning out to be, the cow severing the umbilicus and tying a makeshift knot. And, in time, so the horse and goat don't feel left out, the improvising of a makeshift crib, a harness, a manger, so as to carry the infant with them on their adventures. Such detail shall be added at a later date to add conviction. First, however, they must get the newborn out of the shed. The horse leans his great rump against the door. It is not locked. The hinges squeal for want of oil or tallow. Outside, the smoking ruins of the homestead. The quiet, but for the coals crackling and cooling, and perhaps a solo violin informs them that all is not well. Old Farmer Grogan has gone. In the midst of birth—death. They realize that the sleeping, milk-numb infant is now their responsibility. The four eyes of the three, for one has been blinded, meet. They will continue to run the farm as best they know how. Orwell has gone. Rising to the occasion they return to the shed where they continue to live, eating the straw while the child grows, gains weight, becomes a toddler before their astonished gaze. When the straw is gone the child decides he wants to see the world, so the harness is eventually put to good use. They do not look back at the hayshed, scene of their shared past, their happy times together. They leave with the sun high overhead and vow never to return.

Meanwhile in the distant city the girl has also grown, suckled in the conventional manner. Her mother, unable to cope with the pressures of single parenthood, marries. The stepfather—no, this is getting complicated again. Have it that the mother, for reasons best left to herself, puts the baby up for adoption. The child is sent first to a church orphanage, then later to various foster homes. From these she learns to walk, talk, tie her shoelaces, spit, swear, and clench the muscles controlling her bladder. This last with difficulty. She eats ravenously. Given so many foster parents there is no continuity of upbringing, and certainly no regulation of diet. Strangely, apart from her nails, she eats cloth, she eats blossom and tuberous bulbs, she eats insects from beneath the bark of trees. Once she eats the tongue of her shoe. She grows. Prospers. She contemplates, in due course, kindergarten, primary school, secondary school and university, in that order. Plus post-graduate studies in language acquisition, eating disorders and the effect of maternal deprivation on certain primates. She becomes a highly respected member of her profession. She earns a large salary, although she will be the first to admit that such things mean little to her. There is still a great emptiness in her life that is not filled by love or success. Sadly her story contains no dialogue with which to demonstrate her academic qualifications, nor reveal the impoverished state of her soul.

As stated earlier, both she and the boy, who has now grown into a man with an astonishing predilection for animal mimicry, are destined never to meet. Although their paths may well cross, each remains ignorant of the existence of the other. They grow up with their unusual interests and influences. They grow old. Perhaps one of them is struck down with disease. On lonely winter nights each dream, in some symbolic fulfillment of their fate, of a mysterious figure whose language they do not understand, yet with whom they sense a strange affinity. The ever present Other who seems to hint at an answer to their primal query: Who am I? Who can I expect to be in relation to dot dot dot . . . Perhaps such symbolism is going too far? A longer story would have allowed more satisfactory resolution of such themes. Perhaps even a chance meeting on a wildlife documentary. Luckily for us they have no offspring. Unfortunately their names remain irrelevant, as if to suggest these characters may well serve some higher, universal function. Their identity shall not be disclosed even in the forthcoming sequel concerning the destiny of the horse, the cow, the goat, named respectively, Dobbin, Daisy, and William, one of whom is blinded in a farming accident. You can see the difficulties I have encountered in the telling of this story. The intricate blending of biography and fiction, truth and verisimilitude. I hope such problems as I have attempted to overcome may be ironed out with the later inclusion of detail. The characters themselves I feel have been sufficiently developed so as to give them lives of their own. I recognize the story of the view has been largely neglected, and for this I am sorry . . .

PART TWO

The Republic of North Eastern Victoria

They left through the mist, disappearing between scribbly gums. A vivid ring hovered around the moon's bright eye. A mopoke's cry in the night. The dogs paid foof to their departure, whining and grovelling on the dirt floor. They left before the terrible shriek of metal, and horses screaming came to us over the treetops. It were a frightful sound, made more terrible by our anticipation of it, but also one that made us alert and vinegary. It were as if I could see every little movement in the room. The moths about the lantern, the drip of spilled slape ale. It were like I could sense the ants hesitating at the table edge, the twitching of the teacher's limbs in their bindings.

It were our job to guard the teacher. Me and the women. My name is Barney Benson and I were fourteen years old. I had been placed in charge, which made me feel all hot and peppery. The teacher was trussed like a rodeo steer and I had a mattock handle with which I had been instructed to 'lay about him' if he started up with his strut-speech. I knew the teacher's sweet talking ways being, as he was, the one what taught me my letters and my jawing tacks. He had cut my knuckles open often enough to get my letters straight, so I suppose I must thank him for that, for all the good it did me.

'Barney,' he had gasped when we first trussed him, 'surely you'll not be swept along in this?'

I took much pleasure in plugging his gob with the slops rag. He did not resist. The mattock handle gave me great authority in the matter. Besides, the crowd were in too jovial and rumbustious a mood to pay him heed. All we had to do was wait patiently and then we would be free. This waiting left me hungry and there was not a snattock of grub in the place, nor any sculsh, only the dwindling bottles of white-eye.

Silence outside, as the mist gathered itself. It were like a blanket come down over the night. The mopoke's hoot again. The quiet of bull's-noon, when not even the babbies dare wake. Then came, as we knew they would, the awful sounds of the crash and the poor horses. Soon after came the reports of shots, followed by their echoes stretching across the night's divide. Bogus Harrington, one of the townsmen left behind, said, 'Well lads are we going to let them do all the work?'

'No.'

'Are we going to sit here and miss out on all the fun?'

'No.'

'Then let's lift our pony shanks and get cracking.'

The men, who were all belly full of clamberskull, ran out

into the night armed with bottles and whatever they could lift from behind the bar, leaving me remaining with the women and the teacher. A part of me wanted to be with them, but I was all a-swazz with the importance of the job entrusted to me.

The whipbird snapping of the shots came in a slow and ordered manner. The screams of the horses, one by one, fell silent, although it were a long process. It took a while to put the puzzle together, listening from a distance. One of the women, Mrs Bogus, relieved the stool of her rear, went over to the teacher and pulled the plug from his gob so as to give him some water.

'Put that back,' I ordered.

'Don't you talk like that to me Barney Benson,' she said. 'He teaches our Jenny, of course I'm going to give him some water.'

Now that he had the chance it seemed the teacher's turn to speak.

'Are you all going to stand here while this carnage takes place?'

'Shut it,' I swore.

'Let me loose.'

'Not on your nelly.'

'Drink this,' said Mrs Bogus, holding the tankard to his flepper. He took a good long goblock, spluttering a bit.

'Is this—Is this how you want to be remembered Barney, as an accom—an accomplice to murder?'

'To liberty, you mean,' said I.

I elbowed Mrs Bogus aside and shoved the slops rag back in place. I would have liked to force it down his manky gullet, but not in front of my Mam and the other ladies. My Mam had her hands about a tankard of heel-taps and she were as happy as a pig in gravy. As I said it were all very exciting.

In the distance the shots did not let up.

After some time of this we heard the midwife-gallop of footsteps outside and the door flew open. A red faced, little urf called Jack Jones danced inside causing a great bruzzle, the nerves jumping in his face like a snake at a square dance. All the lanterns flickered.

'Barney, they want the teacher.'

'Eh? Are you sure?'

'Sure as eggs is eggs. They sent me runnin'. They want Mr Curnow.'

I untied the teacher's legs and hauled him to his feet, but left his hands bound behind him. I put on a hat. I did not know what I was preparing myself for.

'Be careful Barney,' called my Ma from her stool, and we left the hotel.

Armed with my mattock handle I made the teacher march before me, following Jack's tracks. We noggled our way up the hill towards the railway and the sound of the kerfuffle. It were slow progress because Curnow with his gammy leg kept slipping on the loose quartz and shale, and could not get his proper wind on account of the rag in his gob.

The shots loudened as we climbed. And the voices. Then the feff of smoke and gunpowder came stronger. The ambush had worked. It were a plan that none of us could wholly believe, but here it was. It might never have worked, but it had. The scene, when we found it, were a complete clowclash with smoke and wreckage and cries everywhere. By cripes it were a mess. The train lay on its roof having tumbled cartwheel-wise from the sundered track on the bend above. Its fall had scoured a clearing through the saplings, halted only by the sturdiest of trees half way down the slope. The couplings of the last two carriages had snapped, sending them further into the scrub to land on their sides. It were like a beast had gouged at the earth looking for ants to tease. The trees stood around like a ring of onlookers at a boxing stoush. What I seen, silhouetted against the light from the blaze in the engine, was the metal men. The great clanking iron men moving methodically step by step down the length of the train. At each window or shattered doorframe they would peer in, then point their Colts into the darkness and fire, two, three, four times. There were screams from within that I realized were not the screams of horses. Two screams, one scream, silence. It was slow work because they had to take turns to reload their revolvers. The men from the town were cheering them on. I seen one hipshot trap trying to crawl from the wreck on broken limbs, only to have a pistol aimed at his temple and the trigger nonchalantly pulled, like a burned sheep being put down after a scrub fire. From the distance it were impossible to tell which iron man from which. I understood it were a devilish scene, but it were not meant to be, and so I had to alter the way I regarded it.

Curnow glunched and chawed his gullet in horror. He did not comprehend what he were seeing. Somewhere he had lost his eyeglasses and his nose holes were widened with the effort of pulling in the air, which were full of smoke and not really ripe for the pulling. From further down the train, in the rear-ward carriages, they were half-heartedly returning fire. Their bullets clanged and gave ricochet off the armoured men into the darkness.

Some of the other townsmen and farmers, who had no armour, were sheltering by the head of the train, the engine of which smoked steadily. The carriages strewn behind it all twisted and crushed like a giant squeezebox thrown down in anger. Not a window had survived. From the rear carriages came the moaning of the injured. Help help, and so on. A pistol shot now and again. There was almost a carnival mood amongst the onlookers, who did not rightly know if they were merely witnesses or now had some deeper involvement that bound them to the moment.

After a while one of the iron men crambled awkwardly over to us. His voice resounding within the helmet as if it were a pulpit-thumping sermon in a pig trough. We could not distinguish his words, only the authority of them. At our confusion he lifted his great helmet. It was Ned, roaring, 'What do you mean you great splay footed spud nosed echidna pricked sons of Irish gombeens this ain't no travelling sideshow either you're with us or you're not and if you're not then vacate the Republic has no need of gawking tinny hunters warming their cockles.'

There was not a breath between his words, which was the way he always talked.

'We're with you Ned,' cried Bogus Harrington from the back of the mob.

I suppose I should not call them a mob anymore because, as events were turning out, they were fast becoming a revolutionary force, an army, albeit a mawmsey one, fuelled by too much grog and the late hour.

'Then for God's sake help us dispatch these low dogs before they recover their senses do you think they won't do the same to you if they get the chance what they've been doing to us all these years past?'

'With what, Ned? We haven't any weapons.'

'With your bare hands,' he bellowed fiercely, 'with the rocks of the field turn their own weaponry on them.'

He indicated the body of a trap lying half out of a splintered window, his hand still clutching a carbine. Bogus Harrington ran forward to snatch it up.

'Whacko!'

Down the length of the train loose shots pinged off the armour of the others, Dan and Joe and Steve. They did not flinch, but continued their own steady work. You could see the good idea that lay behind the armour. It weren't nearly so comical now.

Ned continued, 'Some of you see if you can't get that boiler fire spread to the carriages and some of you track around the scrub for any stragglers we want no likes of McIntyre escaping tonight to raise the alarm.'

'Righto Ned.'

'Don't "righto Ned" me hop to it you toad-eaters.'

The men dispersed and the carnage continued. Ned supervised the operation. Using the traps' own firearms speeded up the dirty work. A small part of me even began to feel sorry for the traps, wounded and injured from the wreck as they were. It were hardly a fair jannocks, but then if the shoe were on the other foot we would not have expected different. Some of the lads were taking real pleasure in giving a bit back to them. There was even laughter. Ned delegated the remainder of the dispatching carriage by carriage. We were no longer witnesses, no fear, we were participants. We were, as Ned reminded us, standing up at last to the oppressors; we were founding fathers of the new Republic. He made us feel strong and privileged and somehow right, and this added to our purpose.

The fire, having been teased from the broken furnace, began to spread through the first carriage, the men shoving burning faggots in through the windows. Curnow writhed in my grip, making little kitteny noises. The smoke billowed upward foretelling a woeful start to the day. I would have preferred it to remain dark a little longer. At the far end of the train the shooting continued. Those horses in the last carriage not killed in the crash were put out of their misery. It were a sad sight all round to see, like shooting fish in a barrel. There was not one that had not been maimed in the tumble down hill. It were in a strange way worse than the crying of men, for none of us cared two hoots for the men. A yelp from one of ours came up the line. Bogus had received a wound to his foot.

'I'll need the flesh-tailor,' he gasped, hopping over to rest by the bole of a tree.

'Crack hardy mate,' echoed Joe Byrne's metallic voice, 'we'll get your missus to suck the bullet out.'

Someone else gave him a slug of nobbler. He were wincing, but happy. He reefed his boot off to examine the hole in him.

The whimpers of the injured were subsiding as the liberating party moved down either side of the train's carcass. Occasionally bullets from within would hiss and zip about their ankles, which is what happened to Bogus. In desperation Curnow managed to work loose his sodden plug and spit it out.

'Enough!' he shrieked, 'Stop! Must you murder all of them?'

A few heads turned, including Ned's great tazzled one, but no one stopped their business. Ned strode over to us, not bothering with the helmet now.

'Must I? Why must I? Must I not rather try to restore the freedom of honest farmers and settlers?'

'This is—this is—barbarous. Must you kill everyone?'

'Yes I must.'

'They can barely crawl.'

'They are milklivered.'

'You—you—' he maffled, 'you are a butcher.'

At that observation I whacked my old teacher about the ear with my mattock handle. His ear split open like an old tomato and he fell down hard. I must say that was a powerful feeling and relieved me of much pent up sensation I had been harbouring. The cuts to the knuckles and so on. Ned stood over him.

'This is the birth of a new Republic Curnow a new beginning the traps'll think twice before they next send a train into our butts and bounds.'

Curnow gave a kelk in reply.

'You call me a butcher,' Ned continued, 'I ask you what Republic was not born of blood? history is written by the victors and I have written this night's page you are witness to it as it is and as it should be stand him up Barney so he can see all.'

I dragged Curnow to his feet; the blood trickled down the side of his turnip.

'What have you to say now Mr Curnow?' Ned looked up at the dark, smoky sky.

'Too many words,' Curnow managed a croak, 'have been spilled in your name Ned Kelly.'

'Will I let him have it again, Ned?' I asked.

'No Barney there's no point there's two hundred dead here Curnow or soon will be what makes you so certain I'll not add you to the pyre?'

'Nothing makes me certain of anything anymore.'

'Do you not see we have won?'

'For what you have unleashed, it is a Pyrrhic victory.'

'A victory for all of that.'

'Your family were scapegoats. People pitied you. Admired you. Now you are an abomination. Pity all of us.'

'You think me a symbol Curnow I aren't no symbol for your squalor I have unleashed nothing for there never was no leash.'

Another shout came from down the line. The spreading fire was getting louder and hotter, lighting up the sky. The bush round about us lay in darkness. I could hear disturbed birds squawking. Dan and Steve Hart in their prodigious armour were dragging a lame trap between them. They were enjoying the dance with the poorly aimed bullets. They had taken off their helmets and their heads looked shrunken in relation to the rest of their size, like a couple of peas in a stew. When they reached us they held up the rag doll that was Superintendent O'Hare. He had been wounded in the hand, and something was amiss with his legs. The feff of conskite reeked from his breeches.

'Look at this. A nice hostage we have here to trade for our Ma,' said Dan.

'I arrest you Ned Kelly,' mumbled O'Hare to much amusement, 'I arrest you in the name of—'

Ned interrupted him, 'You are the captain of an invading force I have a message for you to take back to your superiors.'

He took his Colt and pressed it at O'Hare's forehead and blew his brains out. The rest of him slumped to the ground as Steve and Dan jumped aside.

'Jesus Ned!'

Curnow fell back against me, but I held him up to see what I myself had to. I suppose Ned wanted him to remember and wordify it for all the history books, but Curnow looked numb and flummoxed, like a catfish asleep too long in the mud.

'Make certain of it lads,' Ned called out to his carousing troops, 'dispatch every last one of them there's no turning back now this cannot be left half done spread that fire damn you let's have some warmth here to celebrate this great night's work jump to it my orders will be obeyed.'

There was a cheer from the men. Some of them were armed with pitchforks, some with spades, some with revolvers taken from the troopers.

The fire had stretched through two carriages and would soon engulf the length of the train entire. There had been no shots for several minutes.

'By Jesus this tin can is heavy,' I heard Steve say.

The ground at our feet was soaked with blood or oil or some other vital fluid from the train, it were impossible to tell without dipping your fingers into it. Gazing into the flames the face of every man, including the teacher who was bloodied and weeping, was illuminated in a range of human expression. Many of them honestly thought the world had newly changed. I suddenly felt liversick and sorry for having belted the teacher so hard. I thought to untie his hands.

Someone cried out, 'Three cheers for the Kellys.'

And there were. There was a look of helpless abjection on Curnow's face, who stared at the ground shaking his head a little, and seemed to be pretending it were all a dream.

Two of the farmers picked up O'Hare's body and threw it into the fire. Sparks flew high into the sky, which was dawning towards Whorouly and Myrtleford and the mountains beyond. We had to step back from the flames. The leaves of the gums above us were curling in the heat. It seemed as though the trees had turned their backs on the spectacle like a man toasting his backside for warmth.

'I'm cooking like a turkey in this tin pot,' said Joe Byrne.

They all looked at each other, the founders of this new State, unsure about the magnitude of what it was they had achieved. I heaved a great yawn. I were dead tired. Someone handed Dan a bottle. I was glad that none of the women, my Ma included, were hiding in the shadows behind us, that none of them had crept up from the hotel to observe us at our triumph.

Turning the Other Cheek

My son is an innocent man. It is a measure of how strongly I feel about this, that I am attempting to say things as plainly as possible, but it doesn't always work. I end up sounding like a Methodist minister, which is not so strange because that is what I am. I am too loquacious. Like Dickensian lawyers perhaps, the prophets were also paid by the word. I am the type who calls a spade an earth digging utensil.

It is an affront to all civilized people that an innocent man should be suspected of this terrible thing, let alone tried and convicted. It's like my life has become a dream. What I am here to ask you is this: my son, my Richard—a boy who wept when he saw dead birds by the roadside, how can he be guilty of anything? Over-sensitivity, maybe, but that is hardly a crime. Of what they allege he is as a sparrow in the hand of God.

How do I know? What gives me the confidence to say this?

Why, the way I brought him up. The force of my love for him. For instance, something I have never told anyone: I kept the withered stump of his umbilicus for several years wrapped in a tissue until it mummified, to remind me of that moment in the hospital, the moment as I stood bursting with pride and happiness. Nothing in his background warrants the sort of forensic attention the media has given to it. The raking over of old school photographs, Richard's face haloed within a conspicuous circle. The opinion pieces in the newspaper looking for explanations—this is misguided tub-thumping. They can contort anything they want into the wildest fabrication. Meanwhile the true culprit is sitting back somewhere, laughing in the secrecy of his own crimson sin.

As these cheap journalists camp on my nature strip, slapping their arms against the cold, I see them cooking up headlines like scouts about a bonfire. The first thing they consign to the flames is the truth. It doesn't sell enough papers. I step from my car and, in bloodlust, they surround me, microphones thrust into my face, cameras flashing. My wife begins to cry and it is these photos that make it to page three under the banner: *Parents' Shame.*

How am I to take their lies? How am I to face my congregants as they wonder what on earth it was like in our house that night, once the heavens fell? Well, nothing happened. We went about our business. Our rituals. What happened was that the police arrived. Richard was arrested. They spent a lot of time in his bedroom. Then they took him away. Eventually, a trial. Our little world devastated. That everything can end while we go on sleeping, or mowing the lawn, or preparing breakfast, that is the shame against which my heart riots. I cannot understand why every father is not outraged, because I am so? My wife, Marjorie, thinks I am becoming obsessive about this, but I am not, I am calm and methodical, focused and determined. And in time, I believe, when I am vindicated, the heavens shall be hammered back into their rightful place. Amen.

Now, when I visit my son I see a broken man. Not the son I raised to hold his head up, to be respectful of women and his elders and people of other cultures. I see a man who has been drained of his soul. He sits there in his prison greens at the awful table bolted to the floor, and stares at his hands. I note that Richard looks too thin, too haggard and drawn. Has he been eating properly? It is hard to get him to talk. When he finally opens his mouth he whispers that the other prisoners want me to bring in drugs on my next visit. Drugs. Me? This is absurd. Where would I begin to look?

He can give me the name of a place. I am shocked.

'Why should I do that?'

'Because,' he answers, heavily, 'if you don't they are going to pour boiling water on my cock.'

All about us the conversations are hushed and furtive. I refuse to discuss this business of drugs. In desperation he suggests I can secrete them in my back passage to get past the guards.

I cannot look at him. I am glad when they call an end to the visit.

Each week he stares at his hands and says nothing. Hands with the fingernails all but gone; the cuticles gnawed back, the tan nicotine stains. It is painful to look at them. They are the hands a piano would shrink from in distaste. I tell him how his mother and I are coping with our new lives. Of the congregation. He does not reply. It is as much as I can bring myself to do, to drive the three hours to visit him, to look at his hands, his bitten quicks, then to drive the three hours home. But I do. What else am I for? *I was in prison and ye came unto me.*

My son is a great, if slow, reader. It has taken him six months to read *The Turn of the Screw,* and when the other prisoners ask what he is reading he tells them, I imagine, a book my father recommended. I am trying to keep his mind stimulated during this time of tribulation. This limbo. Oh I know he has a teacher, and a chaplain, I am glad to hear. He talks about them being the only "normal" people in his world. They provide him with reading material, but really there are far more needy souls than Richard's; the illiterate, the addled, the apostate—these people are in greater need of their help. Richard at least has something of an education. He might even be able to assist in the prison chapel with interpretation of the Gospels. They will see that the pestilence of drugs is not the answer. I am not ashamed to say I am proud of him.

I have engaged a Senior Counsel, Mr Luscombe, to contest the appeal proceedings. I cannot afford a QC, and the church synod will not approve funding for what they imply is a lost cause. Faith, hope and love, I remind them. Even Mr Luscombe is not overly optimistic, but he is being paid to fight, to have hope. In my research I was curious to discover certain civil litigants whose motto *We Will Sue* is the kind of never-say-die attitude I detected in Luscombe, and which I am looking for in the pursuit of Richard's exoneration.

I explain to Mr Luscombe the history of Richard's episodes. Certainly he was a melancholy boy. Sport did not amuse him.

Sometimes he would lie in bed all weekend. Once he set his bedding on fire as he lay in it. I hardly need to stress this was an accident. When he met Michelle Nankervis (it is hard for me to think of her name), he brightened up. She seemed to bring him out of himself, although I am sure their 'relationship' was never consummated as such. It would have been Richard's first time if it had, though I do not think so for her, judging by the sort of clothes she used to wear, and the raucousness of her laugh. They went to movies together. They went swimming. I saw happiness in his eyes. Even now, in prison, they describe him, vernacularly, as 'having issues'. Issues. What do they mean? Enough blankets; enough pairs of socks? There is no greater issue than the state of a man's soul. The recovery and dusting off and salvation of it.

I drive the three hours. I look at his hands. I drive back.

I ring his psychiatrist, a Dr Costigan, visiting consultant for Justice Health. Mendacious catatonia, she says over the telephone, is the issue. She tells me that Richard has been observed remaining motionless for hours on end, his skin cold and clammy, his jaw agape, letting the cigarette burn down to his bitten fingers. Or else he stands with his face to the wall for half a day or more, before lying down exhausted on his cement bunk. All this captured by the camera in the observation cell.

It is, according to her assessment, an act.

I recognise this sort of behaviour from his youth, so in that respect I concur with the psychiatrist. He may well be faking it, but to what end? It is a lassitude of the spirit, not the mind, lacking the proper means of meditation. A chapel shared with Muslims and Buddhists and anyone else is as ecumenical as diluted milk.

Without constant reminding and renewal God leaks away, like the air from a punctured tyre. The psychiatrist has prescribed medication. I want to know what sort of medication, but she will not tell me, she says that she is not at liberty to discuss the case any further.

'But I am his father,' I say.

'Yes, but you are not his lawyer.'

And she hangs up.

Outrageous. She does not think that I will have the gumption to look up her credentials and, as it so happens, her business address. But I do. She has not answered my questions sufficiently. I stand in her reception room while Dr Costigan finishes her business with a client. I overhear appointments being made. Then she turns to me, and stares. She knows who I am. The receptionist observes us closely. The borborygmus water cooler gurgles in the corner. Dr Costigan says that while she understands my need to help my son, the matter should really be left up to the professionals.

I say, 'Professionals don't care.'

She adds that since the incident with the boiling water Richard is now better off in protective custody. Everything that can be done is being done. She then says I must never attempt to make contact with her again. If I do then she will have no hesitation but to recommend that Richard be sent to Goulburn as an NA: that is, strict non-association. He will speak to no one; interact with no one. Do I understand? Yes doctor, sorry doctor. I nod obsequiously.

A part of me wonders if that would be so bad, to never have to talk to another person ever again.

When I get home there is a message from Mr Luscombe that Richard no longer wishes me to visit him. He withdraws permission. That is painful. Something else I must offer up.

I have informed Mr Luscombe that the rucksack used in the disposal of the remains is mine. I am the one who asked Richard to buy it for me, hence the CCTV footage of him in the department store making no attempt to disguise himself, or conceal the package which formed such a crucial part of the Crown's case. It indicated, according to the court transcripts which I have read, premeditation. But not if it belongs to me. Mr Luscombe says that my 'putting my hand up' like this will not help Richard. I cannot trade places with him. Of course not, I say, I do not wish to trade places, I did not kill the girl, neither of us did. I asked him to buy the rucksack in order that I might go fishing. What sort of fish? That was clever. I do not know the names of any fish. Camping, then.

Richard's best chance at appeal, says Mr Luscombe, is to pursue the route of madness. He needs to be thoroughly assessed. Not guilty by reason of diminished responsibility. But this would be tantamount to admitting that, even in his diminished state, he still did it. And I know for a fact he did not. He is not capable. A boy who weeps when he sees dead birds by the roadside. Even then, Mr Luscombe continues, this would not secure Richard's release. He would be held at (quaint phrase) the Governor's pleasure, until such a time as society has forgotten all about him and he is somehow deemed fit for freedom.

Which is why I cannot comprehend why Richard's teacher, a certain Mr Fitzmaurice, seems to have swallowed the lies promulgated by the press. His name—easy, Richard told me. His address—somewhat harder than the psychiatrist's to obtain given that he has an unlisted telephone number. Plus, I discover, he is not on the electoral roll. Nor are his domestic details readily available from the ratepayers' register in the Council chambers. There is a suppression order against them. All this smacks a little of celebrity paranoia to me, but Mr Fitzmaurice is no celebrity. He is a no one. Some clever sleuthing on my part (a matter of trial and error) eventually helps me run my quarry to ground. I follow a man based on Richard's description as he leaves the gaol car park and memorise his registration number. It is not necessary. I trail him to a leafy *cul de sac*. I see him go into a house. It is all very ordinary. The name on the mail in the letterbox confirms it. No one can hide from God, not even under a rock, and no one can hide from a father determined on freedom for his son.

I go home and formulate what it is I need to know, what I need this teacher to do. Marjorie calls me for dinner, but I am too preoccupied to eat. My mind too fervid.

I choose my moment to call on him: a sunbright Saturday when I should have been visiting my son. Someone in the neighbourhood is mowing their lawn. It's a comforting sound, like a tipsy bee in a sunroom full of flowers.

I stand on the doorstep looking at the grain in the lintel. It takes me a long time to ring the bell. Suddenly I wonder what I am doing here?

'Yes?' says Mr Fitzmaurice opening the door. He is a prematurely grey-haired man.

I try to tell him who I am. What I want. But suddenly words fail me. They are like bones in my throat. What do I want? I cannot speak. I cough and blow my nose. Pollen in the air. Why am I here? What is it I want? I, I, I want the pain in my heart to go away. I want my old life back. I want the fabric of the torn world to reassemble, or else to disintegrate and fade to dust. What I want is too great for ordinary words. I want to tell him this. I gulp. He can see I am distressed. He also knows who I am. I wipe my eyes.

A deep breath. A breath that resounds in my chest like a diving bell, the weight of the dark ocean pressing in. What I want, to get to the point, is for him, Mr Fitzmaurice, to take a message to my son. A message? Yes, plus a crucifix, blessed especially, to give comfort in this time of . . . in this time of his current situation. Is that too much to ask? My eyes sting with bristling tears.

He studies me.

Eventually he says, 'I cannot do that Mr Medson. That is trafficking.'

'It is a crucifix. A holy icon.'

I show it to him, dangling from its thin chain. Christ's agony.

'You could give this to him yourself.'

'Richard will not let me visit him.'

I hate having to make this admission. The stab of pain.

'Why not?'

'He wanted me to break the law.'

'Mr Medson, there are more appropriate avenues for this. You would need to apply for permission to post it to him, but that is possible . . . How did you find me?'

'I am resourceful. I am also a father who would do anything for his son.'

'Are you prepared to serve the two years if I report you?'

'You would not do that.'

'You seem very confident of what I will or will not do.'

'No, I am not confident. I am desperate.'

The morning is alive all around us.

He says, 'I cannot help you.'

'You don't know how much you have helped me already, by helping my son. Richard has told me the sort of man you are. Your character.'

'That is within the parameters of my work.'

'Do you not believe in justice?' I ask.

'Would that be justice for Michelle Nankervis?'

'Justice for an innocent man wrongly convicted.'

He considers this, 'I am indifferent to justice.'

'Because your son is not languishing in prison.'

'No. Just indifferent. It is not my concern.'

I realise I am not above begging.

Behind him faint music comes from the house, drifting down the hall, resonant. The teacher seems to fill the doorway so that I might not look past him. There is a smell of something cooking. Coffee. The carpet within the threshold is worn.

He takes a breath before announcing,

'Mr Medson, I don't know how you found out where I live. This is completely beyond the norm. Please understand I cannot take anything in for Richard. They will think he put you up to it and punish him.'

He hears a noise in the house behind him and turns his head.

'It is highly irregular,' he continues, clearing his throat, 'for you to receive this from me; it is not the usual channel of communication. I am not, by rights, allowed to talk to you. His lawyer should be the one, but you should probably accept the fact that Richard is not innocent.'

'That is not true.'

'I'm afraid it is true.'

'How do you know? Were you there?'

'Richard told me.'

'That is what they call hearsay.'

'It's as the prosecution proved.'

'Then why would he swear to me, his father, otherwise?'

'Because,' the teacher seems to weigh this up, 'because Mr Medson, he is terrified of you.'

'I am trying to free him.'

'He has been terrified of you all his life.'

'You mean to say he would prefer to stay where he is?'

'He seems reconciled to it.'

'Well, that is madness.'

I do not know what more to say. How to respond? It is absurd. My jawbone is tight and painful, my teeth grinding mercilessly. The dark ocean pressing in. The teacher, this character, looks unshaved. To be frank it looks like he has just got out of bed, and here it is ten o'clock in the morning. I cannot believe what he is suggesting, that my Richard did that to poor Michelle Nankervis. That he put her remains in the rucksack. That he carried her about. A small child appears at the teacher's side and peers around his legs.

'Who's that Daddy?' she asks.

'It's no one, darling. Go back to the kitchen.'

Feeling stunned, the breath in my head, I turn on my heel and half stumble down the steps. The heavens are cerulean, dissipated and lost. Birds sit on the TV antennas. A lawnmower buzzes near by. I trudge back towards the car, so far away, in which my wife, Richard's mother, has been patiently waiting, listening to the radio.

Tooth for a Tooth

E ven though it's raining our book club is still meeting tonight, the third Saturday of the month. Sometimes Patty's friend Bronwyn plays the harp while we eat our dinner making us feel very civilized. Personally I could do with a little less of the musical interlude and a little more quaffing of the Shiraz, a little more giggly chit chat free of the censorship of the men. However I have to accept there are horses for courses, and tonight's horse is under Patty's expert whip.

Amanda is getting out.

We have been meeting for twenty years, long before Amanda joined us. A different person's house each month, give or take the holiday season. There is a core group of about six people, although we have sometimes swelled to twice that. Amanda was a stalwart regular who certainly loved her literature. I think tonight it will be a small turn out. The rain. Over the years, however, we have prevailed. All those books. All that conviviality. It certainly beats what the company of our various husbands has to offer. I admit there is something to be said for their monotony, their routine stability; it's just that I forget what it is at the moment. I get the sense that they, the husbands, are slightly envious of the regularity of our meetings. The effervescence we bring home, and which takes a day or two to fade. They resent their irrelevance, and this comes across in sarcasm.

'For Heaven's sake Tony,' I say to Tony when he makes his usual objections, 'we only meet once a month. You meet with your buddies every weekend.'

'That's different.'

'Why is it different?'

'Because I don't walk out without—without—adapting for the needs of the other members of the household.'

'You.'

'If you like.'

'Adapting?'

'Yes.'

'You mean leaving your dinner in the oven.'

'If you like.'

'Get your own dinner. Once a month. It won't kill you.'

Tony is putting on a good display of umbrage.

'Well what do you talk about, at these special meetings of yours?'

'This month's book.'

'And all the gossip.'

'Yes Tony,' I sigh, reaching for my keys, 'That's all we do. Gossip about you.'

You see what I have to contend with.

This month there are only four of us, although it's always a good excuse to get together and chew the fat. Also to experiment with recipes for which our husbands would not be willing guinea pigs. Tonight it's Asian infused swordfish with greens, (Patty's choice) and of course the latest Booker winner, which I admit I struggled through, and in the end skipped to the last chapter. Nevertheless it is very stimulating to discuss the issues raised by the latest Booker winner. Tony's opinion wouldn't amount to a burp.

I am the first to arrive at Patty's house with my contribution, balsamic beans and a bottle of Chardy. The sensor lights guide me up the drive. Her garden looks good, even at night. The doorbell plays a little allegro. We kiss. Patty already has a tumbler of plonk with her lipstick at the rim. The cleaner has been, so the house looks particularly sparkly. There is a new painting on the feature wall, which Patty pointedly ignores. The fruit bowl is full. There are Gerberas on the table. Soon Gina arrives and we have a quorum. We are well on the way, cooking up a storm, discussing plot points and character development over biscuits and Brie. Gina opens a bottle and catches up with Patty in no time. You'd have to say that sometimes our book club floats on a sea of alcohol.

The doorbell trills again. It's Tanya. She's always the last. We all love her, even though she has six sleepers in each ear and a rhinestone stud in her nose. I sometimes wonder if her head jingles when she shakes it? And how does she sleep with all that metal digging into her? Apparently there is a tattoo somewhere on her person, although I have never seen it. As she comes in with a Pyrex casserole dish under her arm and an agonized look on her face the laughter falls like dark matter at our feet.

'What's happened?' Gina asks.

'Have you had an accident?' Patty asks.

'You look as though you've seen a sprite,' I say.

'You haven't heard?' Tanya says, putting her dish down. Her raincoat drips on the polished floor. 'No. Obviously not. It's Amanda. She's coming.'

The air in the room suddenly chills. Actually I had heard, but I'd been hoping the whole issue would just go away.

I see I am going to have to explain about Amanda.

But first, 'When did she get out?' Gina asks.

'A fortnight ago.'

We all pause to register this fact and, frankly, measure it.

'Where is she living?' Patty asks, looking around at her furniture.

'With her mother.'

'My God, that woman must be nearly eighty.'

'Well,' says Tanya, 'she has nowhere else to go.'

'I thought she was never supposed to get out,' says Gina.

'No,' Tanya explains, 'She was eligible for parole a year ago, but they held her back.'

'Oh my God,' Patty says again, and this just about sums up the new mood in the room. The latest Booker winner sits in my bag, heavy as a brick.

Amanda was a member of our group almost from the beginning. Even afterwards, when she was in gaol she used to write us letters giving her opinion on the issues raised in whatever book we happened to be reading. It was strange to read those letters, as if what had happened was a figment, something that took place only in the newspapers. Initially I wondered how she knew what book we were reading, until Tanya explained that she had been writing to Amanda, giving her all our news. She was like a pen pal, Tanya said, except that Amanda's letters had little to say. Nothing ever happened. Mostly her letters were recollections of the past, or yearnings for the trivia that swirled about the whirlpool of the book club. When we learned of this we said, 'Please give her our regards. Say hello from us. Wish her well,' although no one asked for the address so we could write to her ourselves. I had my reasons. I'm sure we all did.

As the years went by marriages came and went, various members of the book club fell away. Enough time passed that it just became inconvenient to think about Amanda. Her husband, Owen, had gone. It was like she'd been swallowed by the past and that terrible time was now over, thank goodness. Everyone had their own lives to be getting on with. One day Tanya declared that she was going to visit Amanda in the prison. That certainly got the tongues wagging. Tanya asked if I would like to go with her, it was Amanda's birthday after all, but as with the letters, I cooked up some excuse for which I am now ashamed. Something to do with Tony.

'Here? Tonight?' Patty asks, the apprehension in her voice taut as an elastic band.

'Bronwyn's bringing her.'

'I don't know if I can have that woman in my house.'

She looks around for moral support. There is plenty.

'Why?' Tanya asks.

This is a good question and I look to Patty because I am not sure what the answer is.

'Why?' Tanya repeats. 'It's Amanda. You remember Amanda. She was your bridesmaid. She's a member of the group. She's one of us.'

'I am *not* like her,' Gina takes a big swig from her tumbler. No one has thought to pour a glass for Tanya, who shrugs off her raincoat and hangs it on the back of a chair. Gravity helps form a little puddle beneath it.

'Why didn't you let us know?' Patty asks.

'I only just found out myself.'

'But you've been in contact with her. You knew she was getting parole.'

It does not matter who says this, we are all thinking it.

At this moment Patty's son, Nick, strolls into the room, like an unexpectedly big wave at the beach. He peers into Patty's saucepans bubbling away on the stove. He is a tall, striking boy of about sixteen, with shoulder length hair. He is the sort the girls are swooning over, if girls ever swoon these days. It is as if all the middle-aged ladies in the room are invisible to him.

'What's for dinner Mum?'

'That's for us,' snaps Patty, 'Your father is taking you and your sister out for Indian.'

'Mad,' says Nick, replacing a saucepan lid and strolling—*cruising*, is that the word? out of the room. All the footprints on the beach wiped clean behind him.

'I knew she was *eligible* for parole,' says Tanya, 'I didn't know she was actually going to get it. I was as shocked as you. She rang me out of the blue.'

'Why didn't you tell us?'

'I'm telling you now.'

Even I can hear that Patty is chastising Tanya as if it's all her fault. Her lovely Asian infused swordfish evening is turning into a disaster.

'I thought she was locked away forever,' says Gina, who suddenly looks much plumper and red faced than she did a minute ago. 'I mean, I never actually thought of her getting out. What did they call her? She had some label.'

'She *was* what they call a forensic patient,' says Tanya, 'She's not anymore.'

The pots are steaming on the stovetop. Patty flicks on an extractor fan, which hums smoothly.

'What does that mean?' I ask.

'It means she's crazy,' says Gina, topping up her tumbler to the brim.

'*Was* crazy,' says Tanya, 'at the time of the offence. It was a mitigating factor.'

'Oh for goodness sake,' snaps Patty, 'Stop pussyfooting about the bush. She strangled her own baby. She put her hands around her neck and squeezed until the baby went blue.'

There is silence. That cuts straight to the point, the one we have been trying to block out of our minds all these years. At the time the newspapers dot-pointed: *Young mother found guilty. Fourteen-month-old baby. Infanticide. History of post-natal depression.* Other grisly details besides. There was a photo of Amanda in handcuffs. It wasn't the Amanda we knew.

'I'm not having that person in my living room,' says Patty, 'sitting on my chaise lounge.'

We consider the inflexibility of this remark.

'Do you think she should still be punished then?' asks Tanya.

'Of course.'

'Our friend, Amanda. You think she should still be punished.'

'For what she did. Yes.'

'She killed her own baby. A long time ago. When you were a new mother, without sleep, tits red raw and nipples split, not, as they say, in your right mind, didn't you ever want to strangle your baby?'

'If I did I never acted on it,' says Patty.

'Didn't any of you?' Tanya asks.

'Yes,' I say, 'I felt like that. Quite a bit.'

'Well at least you never acted on it.'

'No. I was too tired.'

'None of us realized how depressed Amanda was,' Tanya says. 'Imagine how guilty she must feel. That's not going to go away. Don't you think she's been punished enough? Because according to the courts she has. That is, according to *society.* Are you saying we should carry on with the punishment?'

From beyond the kitchen a teenage voice wails, 'Mum, there's something wrong with the telly.'

Patty says, 'That child was the same age as Nick. We used to baby sit for each other.'

'Can't you remember the baby's name?' asks Tanya.

140

We have to think.

'Claire,' I recall, 'My perfume made her sneeze.' Then something I remember, 'Her fontanel took a long time to close up.'

'Don't you think Amanda might need some support right now?'

'I think she's got a lot of cheek,' says Patty, 'intruding back into our lives.'

'You all sent your regards to her,' Tanya continues, 'when I wrote and when I visited. Didn't you mean it? Do we tell her you didn't mean it?'

Another silence.

'What was that like? Visiting her,' I ask, knowing my curiosity is coming a bit late in the day.

'Awful,' says Tanya, 'If you have an under-wire bra you have to take it off before you go through the metal detector. You have to talk in a quiet voice or else they terminate your visit. I tried to give her a photo, you know from that day we all went down to Inverloch. She said I wasn't allowed to give her photos. They'd be confiscated. I had to post it to her.'

'I remember that day,' says Gina.

'You're forgetting the salient point,' says Patty, crisply. 'She killed her own child.'

'And you still want to go on judging her. After all these years, Patty. She's done her time. She's been punished.'

'How do you know she's not still crazy?' Gina asks.

'I guess the people who decide these things reckon she's not.'

'That she's fit for society.'

'Something like that.'

'What do they know? Don't you remember that funeral?'

'Yes I do,' Tanya says, 'But now she's out. She's been condemned. She's been locked up for sixteen years. Isn't that punishment enough? For your satisfaction.'

'Is that all? Just sixteen years, for a whole life?'

'What does she look like?' I ask.

'Well she hasn't had the tweaking that we've had. The question is do we still judge her?'

'I would have thought,' says Patty, 'that the question is why should we forgive her?'

'Well her husband will never forgive her,' says Gina.

'Ex-husband.'

'Isn't that enough un-forgiveness in one person's life, without the rest of us getting in on the act? Imagine the energy it must take to sustain that. It's not as though she's walking back into a nice clean life. It won't be easy for her. Do you want her to fail?'

'Do you just want us to forget all about it?' asks Patty.

The rain is making a quiet noise like rice on the windows.

'We don't have to do either,' I say, 'We only have to give her a feed. Maybe take her shopping.'

'Exactly,' says Tanya, 'What else are we for?'

'What if she's not rehabilitated?' Gina asks, her eyes slightly glazed. 'What if she tries the same thing again?'

'I'd like to see her try and take on Nick,' I joke.

'Don't be flippant,' says Gina.

'That's exactly what I thought at the time,' says Patty, 'What if she'd been baby-sitting both of them?'

'Mum this bloody DVD player doesn't work,' Nick's voice

comes from the other room. A living, breathing, human voice followed by a thump as he gives the TV a whack.

Gina says, 'Is that a new painting Patty?'

We all look at the painting for a moment.

'So we have to ask ourselves,' Tanya says, 'before the doorbell rings again. I'm in this boat with you. I don't know if I'd like her sleeping in my spare room. At least I have a spare room. She has nothing. No money. No job. She doesn't even know how to use a mobile phone. The question is do we accept her? Here, tonight. Or don't we?'

'She's not like us,' says Gina.

'Gina, you drive home after what you've had to drink and knock someone off their bicycle and you'll wind up exactly like her. I know I gave my son a clout about the ear when he was five or six and being a complete bastard. It's just that Amanda went too far.'

'Stop making excuses for her,' says Patty, 'you didn't have to write to her. Implying she would be welcome. You've caused all this.'

'Well I don't know about you,' says Gina, affronted at the allusion to how much she's drinking, 'but I just couldn't stand to be in the same room as her. I'd be sick.'

'You might be sick,' says Tanya, 'if you eat whatever's burning there on the stove. Do we forgive Patty for that?'

'My swordfish!' Patty squeaks, jumping up.

She works the stove like the controls of a nuclear reactor. None of us laugh.

'Patty might kill us all before the night's out.'

'But Patty wouldn't mean it,' says Gina, beginning to slur her words. 'I don't know. I don't know what the answer is. What would we talk to her about? How was gaol? What have you been up to these last fourteen years? Read any good books? How do you deal with someone in that situation? I don't know. I need to go to the loo . . . ' Gina struggles to her feet, continuing, 'Patty, I do like that painting . . . I guess . . . I guess it's a question for us all.'

And we watch her glide like a tug boat up the passage. At that moment the doorbell sounds and we all freeze, before assuming, as one, our brightest, happy masks.

A Day in Court

'Fore!' Toby Luscombe SC calls even before he has teed off from the fourteenth. His ball slices high to the right before bouncing once on the fairway, then off into the rough. A couple of groundsmen on an idling tractor are waiting for us to pass through. Golf: a good walk spoiled, so said Mark Twain, or was it Oscar Wilde? I always forget, spoiled or ruined. It makes you wonder how someone so clever could get it so wrong. It is a saying with which, you will understand, I profoundly disagree. Golf is civilization's sweet pinnacle. Drug smuggling its nadir.

Toby Luscombe doesn't look too upset by it. In fact he is looking cock-a-hoop, even after such a poor shot. He replaces the divot, which has flown a couple of metres—a bird made of mud.

'Go easy on the backswing,' I tell him before taking my own shot, straight as a die, down the line like a meteorite, or a hailstone ricocheting off a car bonnet. Toby is wearing shorts, a kind of yellow tartan like a liquorice allsort, and a paisley shirt if you please, as far from his barrister's gown as he can get. His hair, thinning now, is liberated from the humidity of the horsehair wig where, as far as I can tell, it customarily should be at this time of the day. The breeze toys with it like the loose stuffing of a mattress, what is that stuff? Kapok, yes.

The course looks gorgeous this morning after the mist has lifted. The trees thick with October blossom, and the shaved greens manicured into billiard felt. I have seen pictures of Buddhist monks concentrating on putting a golf ball with a pure, golden focus. The mind emptied, the world reduced to that singular moment of harmony and oneness. I know the feeling. A perfect morning for it, despite a water pipe on the sixth, which has burst blowing out a bunker. The groundsmen will have a job shovelling out the sand so as to find the leak and fix it. Toby's earlier drive from half way down the fairway has narrowly missed one of them, who then trod the ball into the slush, so that Toby had to drop a shot digging it out. He wasn't happy about that, but it doesn't last long. It is too nice a day.

We stroll down the fairway where, last month, two lady golfers were attacked by a big (we think amorous) kangaroo. They'd had to beat it off with seven irons and later showed me the scratches back in the clubhouse. The groundsmen are now on kangaroo alert as well as everything else they have to do. It's a wonder they haven't been to the union. I look around but there appears to be no immediate danger from the wild life. Quite the opposite. Nothing but flirting birds and sunshine and those two fellows looking at us from the bushes like a couple of lions at the edge of the savannah.

I can tell they are up to something, drinking perhaps, certainly skiving off digging out that bunker.

Toby is whistling. You hardly ever hear people whistle anymore.

'You sound happy Toby,' I say when he catches up to me, wheeling his buggy with its coppice of wedges and drivers and putters.

'I am, Phil.'

Toby chips out of the rough.

'Shouldn't you be in court?'

'I am. Court is in session.'

Another shot and I am by the flag. My ball rattles in the cup. Par. Toby takes a few extra shots to get on the green.

'You're slapping at it,' I say. 'You've got to guide and glide. Be Zen.'

He tries to be Zen, his kapok drifting in the air, the air all honey blossom and birdsong. Toby lines up his putt by sighting along his club as if it is a billiard cue.

'I wish those birds would shut up,' he mutters.

We stop for a drink at the bubbler on the fifteenth tee. There is moss and bird cack in the basin from all the plovers and starlings that inhabit the course.

'Well that's rather disgusting,' says Toby. 'That's like the snail in my bottle of ginger pop, Phil. I ought to sue your ass, as the Americans say.'

Luckily I have a few bottles of Evian. No snails.

'So how come you've got the day off Toby? Stay of proceedings? Or whatever you call it?'

'No,' he says, 'Extradition hearing. You don't want to know

about it. I've got these two Mexican fellows, the ones who busted out of Parklea. You may have read about it.'

'I think I saw that on the news. A truck, was it?'

'Very dramatic. Driver left the keys in the ignition. *Carpe diem.* In they jumped and quick as you like crashed through the gate. And let me tell you they made one hell of a mess of the gate. And furthermore it's a big bloody thing too.'

'Where there's a will,' I say. 'Mexican, were they?'

Toby nods, bending over his ball.

'One of these cartels. Sixty kilos. Hidden in surfboards. The Americans want them for an even bigger haul in California. The whole thing's a train wreck. Enough to put them away for fifty years. They certainly do not want to be going back there.'

I whistle through my teeth, but for different reasons. I cannot quite get my head around the figures he is expounding. Sixty kilos, fifty years. Toby has some zinc cream on his nose, which makes him look a little clownish. He mops his brow with an ordinary looking handkerchief.

Sometimes there is no place more pleasant than a golf course on a sunny Tuesday morning after the mist has lifted. Even with the mist it is pretty nice. The fairways like rivers of milk lined by trees. I should know. I'm a golf instructor. I see it in all weathers. Do what you love, I say. An image of Heaven might be something not unlike a golf course on such a morning. Those monks knew they had cottoned on to something. In a fine shot, when it all comes together, you can see Zeno's paradox—the stillness of flight—arcing across the parabola of heaven. Oneness. Most golfers don't understand that. They just want to get their handicap down. Mark Twain and Oscar Wilde can laugh all they like.

'Didn't they get to Melbourne or somewhere?' I ask, returning to the moment.

'Yes, they must have had accomplices. But Melbourne isn't far enough. Now they want to contest extradition proceedings. I guess they'd rather face twenty-five years here with a chance of parole than fifty in California.'

'Wow.'

'All I have to do is get an adjournment. Then we'll work out a way to stay proceedings and put the whole business on the back burner. They do have escape charges to answer.'

'Nice work,' I say, 'What do you charge for yakka like that?'

I am joking, but he takes me at my word, deadpan.

'Two hundred thousand.'

'For a day's work?'

'An hour's work. Judge Hennessy loves to adjourn things. A great procrastinator, Judge Hennessy. Friend to the underpaid barrister.'

'Two hundred thousand for an hour's work. That's worse than my plumber,' I plunge the needle of my tee into the turf of the fifteenth. I place a Spalding in its little supplicant's cup, upturned like the skull cap of an acorn.

'When are you due?'

Toby glances at his wrist.

'About now.'

'What?'

'Yes, the cartel wetbacks will probably be in the holding cells as we speak.'

I think Toby enjoys using a phrase like *cartel wetbacks*.

'Have they paid you yet?'

'Oh yes. All settled in advance. It's a seller's market.'

'Are you telling me that some Mexican drug lords have paid you two hundred grand to represent them in court and you're out here in your tartan shorts playing golf?'

'That's correct. You are my witness.'

I cannot believe my ears. A rosella cracking gum nuts is being harried by a lone wattlebird.

'Aren't you a little worried, Toby, that the Mexican drug lords might be a little peeved and come asking for their money back?'

'Nope.'

Toby sets his ball on his tee, upturned like the face of a crocus to the sun, or upturned perhaps like a fairy's begging bowl. I'm getting carried away. Too much time on my hands.

'Why not?'

'Because they're going to be extradited. Whether I contest it or not.'

'But they've already paid you.'

'Human effluent, Phil. Don't waste your pity. They won't need the money where they're going.'

'Wealthy human effluent by the sounds of it.'

'Yes. The Americans dearly want them back.'

'What about when they get out?'

'When they get out I'll be 106. Just about ready to retire. *Caveat emptor*, Phil, first rule of jurisprudence, *caveat emptor*.'

Toby has a few practice swings, and then steps up to the tee.

'Fore!'

He drives his ball straight down the fairway, which is a dogleg, par five, a much better shot, the ball vivid in the sky.

'Nice work.'

'I know,' Toby says, looking around at the lush, leafy world. 'Look at us Phil, a beautiful sunny day, birds singing all over the place, a nice bonus in my pocket. Both of us getting paid to hit a little white ball around the paddock. You wouldn't be anywhere else for quids.'

Better, certainly, than a holding cell waiting for your lawyer to turn up, I imagine, however I cannot argue with his eloquence.

Toby is looking particularly pleased with himself.

'I'll even shout you lunch on the nineteenth.'

I take my shot, mind emptied, though not quite at one with itself, and we set off after our balls. The groundsmen, lurking in the bushes, wait for our shots before revving the engine of their tractor and darting across the fairway. The trailing mower chatters and grass sprays up behind in a green wave. They disappear into the trees on the opposite side of the fairway. As Toby approaches his ball he sees that it has been run over and chopped into pieces by the mower. I do not tell him that they probably did it on purpose. They do it all the time. A good walk spoiled. He will have to drop another shot.

'Bastards,' he says.

Dictation

The alert states that on no account should female staff see this person alone. I shall call this person G, out of respect for his privacy. I don't see why male staff should be exempt from this general warning, however it seems to be acceptable that I am left on my own with him. Although we are not entirely alone—I suppose that's the get-out clause—there are other students in the room, smirking into their whiskers. As for the room itself, the setting, there is not much to be said about that. It is what they call non-descript. The window, and what is beyond it, is much more beguiling.

G comes in and sits down. He wants to dictate a letter. That is within my province. I can justify time devoted to that. Forgiveness is not within my province, and nor is judgment. I keep thinking of the old children's rhyme: Dictation dictation dictation / three sausages went to the station / One got lost and one got squashed / and one had a big operation.

I give the others some work to be going on with. G can neither read nor write, so it is a relatively easy matter for me to transcribe what he says. Small measure of achievement. The pedagogical scaffold is not great down here.

This is what he says, 'To my baby Janine, how are you my baby? I hope work is treating you well. I hope you're not too stressed out and that I am not the cause of your stressing out—read that back.'

I finish scribbling the sentence. I read it back. I keep my voice low, out of respect for his privacy, so that the others cannot eavesdrop; however I know they can hear everything. Because it is a personal letter and because I have been trained in the correct composition of personal letters I have written: Dear Janine.

'No I didn't say that, you're making me sound like a wanker. I said to my baby Janine. Just write down what I say.'

I am mindful of the warning that appeared amongst my emails this morning. Why would they write such a thing? I edit with my trusty red, pedagogical pen. He continues, 'My baby, I hear that you smashed up Eddie Gallante's house the other night. I hope, my baby, you didn't smash it up too bad. There's always a mess when a house gets smashed up. I heard you had to have stitches. My baby, you're the most beautiful girl I ever seen. I wish I could be there to kiss your stitches better.'

One of the other students sniggers.

'I know my baby it's hard out there trying to bring up two kids on your own and I'm—read that back.'

'Have you finished the sentence?'

'Just read it.'

I read it. Unedited.

In my professional letter-writing capacity I offer a suggestion, 'You seem to be saying "my baby" a lot.'

'Of course I am, she's my baby isn't she? What are you sayin'?'

'Nothing,' I hold up placatory palms, 'They're your words.'

I leave the scaffold on the ground. I am slightly relieved there is a table between us. A nondescript table. He continues; his voice lowered so it is hard for me to hear him.

'I hope and pray my baby that you can learn not to listen to other people's problems. You know how you can't even stand to see a squashed snail without feeling sorry for it. I know how you like to be involved in your brother's life, but he's old enough to make his own decisions the filthy maggot. I want you to try and be strong and to stop bringing everyone else's worries home with you and—read that back.'

My hand is aching from the sprint of trying to keep up. My writing is decidedly rushed and sloppy. The 'e's I hardly recognize. I read it back.

'What's that word?'

His finger backtracks in the text. He agitates a pen in his other hand, as if in sympathy with the toil of mine. His fingers twitch as if they are writing ghost words.

'That word is *squashed*,' I say, 'as in "squashed snail".'

'I told you just to write down what I say.'

He thumps the table with his fist. On the table is the note pad. The point of his biro penetrates fifteen sheets of foolscap (I count them later) and leaves a little crater in as many again. I know he's not mad at me *per se*. I'm doing him a favour. Quality time. I have to remember that the (likely) reason he cannot read or write is that his brains have been frazzled by a life long cocktail of substances not designed for human consumption, but when did that ever stop anyone? (Polemic, sorry.) Neither judgment nor forgiveness.

'That is what you said.'

'Did I? Squashed snail? That's a fuckin' stupid thing to say.'

'Do you want me to take it out?'

'No, leave it. It'll keep her guessin'. It's just a funny lookin' word. Write this down, quick before I forget: my baby remember that time you come to visit me and you said that three or four years is not too long to wait and that you would wait for me, well I remember that clear as yesterday, I hope you do too. I'm just reminding you of your beautiful promise which gives me hope because you know you can take my hope and crush me like a bug any time you want. You know I love you and want you to be the best person you can be and—read that back.'

I finish the sentence. I do not alter a word. G's tongue plays in the gap where a tooth once was.

He goes on, 'It's just that my baby I know there's nothing I can do while I'm in here, I can't help you with the bills or anything, but it's because I love you so much and I can't stand to think of those putrid fuckin' dogs sniffing around you my baby and laying their stinking fuckin' hands on your skin. Be strong baby for our sake. I know it's hard, but that's because it's hard—read that back.'

I do. I wonder what Janine will think of this, but I don't offer an opinion. My learning curve is steep and swift.

'What else do you think I should say?' he says.

'People sometimes ask about the weather.'

'Fuck that.'

'Sometimes they say what they've been doing.'

'I ain't been doing nothing—hey, put that in—my baby I been doing nothing except sitting on my arse thinking about you—is that a song?'

'I don't know. It should be.'

'What else should I say?'

'It's your letter. I don't want to put words in your mouth.'

'You're the fuckin' teacher for fuck's sake, what fuckin' good are you?'

I meet his eye for a moment, then back to the carpet, (nondescript).

'That's a good question.'

'Do you think I should tell her I love her?'

'You've said that.'

'Okay. Wait, I've got it. My baby Janine, baby, I'm so proud that you have nearly finished your training course. You will make a beautiful nurse. You'll be able to take out your own stitches, and mine too if I have any, and my baby I promise you if thatTAFE teacher ever asks you out for a drink again then you can tell him as soon as I get my parole I'm gunna come around and stomp his fuckin' head until the concrete bleeds—'

'I don't know if that's really appropriate for a love letter.'

'No? What was I sayin'? Fuck, now I've lost my thought.'

His leg shakes furiously under the table. The pen twirls in his fingers, the fingers stained dark with nicotine. His breath. I can see that the others in the room are grinning at us. Either they have finished their work, or else we are more entertaining.

'Have you finished?' I ask.

'No fuck ya, just write this down—it's because I love you my baby, I know I stress you out, but if I do can you tell me and I'll try not to be the cause of all your—what's that word? Yeah—your anxiety. You know me my baby, just tell me to pull my head in, I miss you so much but if I ever hear of you playin' the field again leavin' your two beautiful babies on their own in the house all night then I'm gunna cut your face up with a razor—'

'You can't say that.'

'Why not?'

'That's a threat.'

'It's not a threat. She knows I'm joking.'

'It doesn't sound like a joke. It's threatening and it's hardly the right thing to put in a letter to your girl. If the screws see that you won't get parole.'

I must be feeling pretty bold to be saying this. The table between us. His tongue at work in the tooth hole.

'I'm nearly finished,' he says, 'I just wanna get this outa the way then I'll go.'

'Hey teach,' calls one of the others, here on remand, 'can I have a pencil and a pencil sharpener and a rubber and a note pad?'

I ignore him.

'Hey teach.'

'My baby, it's because I'm doing all these head-miles, I can't sleep anymore, I love you so much and—'

I have stopped writing. My hand is on strike.

'You've said that.'

'Fuck ya, you've made me lose my thought again.'

'Listen,' I put the pen down, gently, 'you tell a girl you love her in a letter like this and she'll be very happy. She'll be happy that you've made the effort to write to her.'

'Yeah?'

'Minus all the angry stuff.'

'What angry stuff?'

I make judiciously with the red pen.

'This stuff. You copy out what's left in your own handwriting and she'll be very pleased with you.'

'Why can't I just send her this?'

At this juncture, if there were a clock, it would loudly tick.

'Because she'll see what's been crossed out, but more importantly she'll have a love letter written in my handwriting and that kind of defeats the purpose.'

'Eh? What are you sayin'? Are you an idiot? What's a porpoise got to do with anything?'

'You just copy it out.'

'That's a lot of work.'

'I know.'

'Will I get a certificate?'

'She's your girlfriend.'

'What sort of car do you drive?'

'That's not important.'

'Is it a Subaru? I bet it's a Subaru . . . What else should I say?'

'You could talk about the weather.'

'Nah. Too poofy.'

'You could tell her how nice you think her hair is.'

'What would be the point of that? Her fuckin' hair, it's just hair.'

'Then you could just sign off.'

'But everyone'll know it was me. I only want her to know.'

That silent clock.

'Probably. It's just a formality. Most letters end like that. You can leave it blank if you like.'

'What the fuck should it matter, she can't read either. She'll have to get someone to read it to her.'

I take a deep breath.

'Are we done?'

'Done. Thanks. Appreciate it. I'll write it out later. Have you got an envelope?'

'No.'

He takes his precious pages and leaves. I feel slightly sullied that my handwriting, with its clumsy 'e's, is walking out the door in G's possession. I flex my stiffened fingers. I look around the room and wonder what it would take to describe it, to capture it, but it's beyond me. It has a door. The key to it is in my pocket. I tell myself there must be an easier way. The shadow of the grill at the window spreads across the floor like a wedge of honeycomb, the milky, winter sunlight filtering through it, as if it knows it doesn't belong here.

The Agreed Facts

HER HONOUR: David Harold Russick you are to be sentenced here for the crimes of kidnapping; also wounding with intent to murder, to wit one Anna Marie Gilfoyle. These offences are against s 27 and s 86(2b) respectively of the Crimes Act, and carry a maximum penalty of twenty five years imprisonment.

The sentence to be imposed is to commence from the date of the offence, being also the date of the arrest of the offender, namely 14 February 2014. The utilitarian worth of your early guilty plea is commensurate with an approximate value of ten percent. This has been duly taken into account and shall be addressed shortly.

These are the agreed facts:

The offender and victim had been involved in a de-facto relationship for four years preceding the offence. This relationship, as we have heard, was both passionate and tumultuous. A relationship to which, I note, the victim persisted in returning. Exactly why, has not been elucidated, a phenomenon which has broader social application than the events of this matter. We have heard testimony as to the frequency with which neighbours complained about noise coming from the house. I note also an Apprehended Violence Order which was rescinded at the behest of the victim in July of 2012.

That the media has labelled this a *crime passionnel* seems to me to beleaguer the point, that first and foremost there was a crime. The passion does not concern us here, unless in terms of motive. There is no exculpation. The deterioration of the relationship was perhaps inevitable, and finally reached the point of no return in January of 2014. The lease on the rental property the victim and offender shared (72 Clyde Street, Doncaster South) had come up for renewal and this provided an opportune time for Ms Gilfoyle to vacate both the premises and the relationship, which had soured irredeemably. She intended to wipe the slate clean. In the interim she had moved in with her parents in Mitcham, and continued to work as a secretary in a conveyance office. The financial debt owed her by the offender she was prepared to yield as the price of removing herself from what she had decided was an untenable situation. In short: a mess. The flurry of intimidatory and manipulative emails and phone messages is evidence of this burgeoning dysfunction.

Reluctantly Mr Russick agreed that he would be absent from the premises on the day of 14 February 2014 in order to allow the victim to return and pack her things. She was particularly concerned to secure some fragile glassware which had sentimental value for her. Ms Gilfoyle had arranged for her father to assist with the removals. He was due to arrive at twelve o'clock with a small truck.

However, when the victim appeared at the premises with some boxes she discovered the offender still *in situ*. He was seated on the lounge, an item of furniture she proposed to take. The offender's presence at the house was effectively an ambush, albeit not an unexpected one. There was some discussion as to the possibility of repairing the relationship in manner similar to that already alluded to, namely Ms Gilfoyle's returning to the seat of her abuse. The familiar pattern of forgiveness and reconciliation. Such discussion included the following exchange.

The victim stated, 'You said you wouldn't be here.'

The offender said, 'We need to talk this through.'

The victim said, 'There's nothing more to talk about.'

The offender said, 'But I love you.'

The victim said, 'That's too bad.'

The offender said, 'If I can't love you then no one else shall.'

The victim said, 'Don't be stupid.'

There was some further dialogue in this vein, ominous in retrospect. They spoke of various alternatives, relating to the rental lease and also the bond, (Ms Gilfoyle's share being an amount of six hundred dollars, although no argument has been brought forward to suggest a motive of greed). Ms Gilfoyle proceeded to pack her belongings while the offender remained seated on the lounge. His presence during such activity must have been disconcerting to say the least. Occasionally he would offer commentary such as, 'You can't take that,' or 'That's mine,' or 'Don't you dare,' from which we can infer with the benefit of hindsight an escalating level of tension. Otherwise the offender merely sat and read the newspaper—said paper with which the victim was trying to wrap the glassware.

At some point the victim's phone rang. Her father was running late. The victim informed him that Mr Russick was still present and she would therefore need a few more minutes alone while they discussed the division of affects. As we have heard Mr Gilfoyle's attitude towards the offender has been sustained as inadmissible. He, to all intents and purposes, proceeded faster. Ms Gilfoyle continued packing. There were several boxes stacked near the front door. Throughout this sequence of events the offender did not offer to help carry any of the chattels. An attitude can be inferred from such omission, if one were needed, which does address the issue of motive.

At some later time she tried to determine if her father had arrived. As she was unlocking the front door the offender seized her from behind, pulling her away from the door and stabbed her several times in the back with a knife. Note the photographic evidence of the offensive wounds to the offender's fingers, the likely cause of which has been elucidated by medical testimony. The fact that the knife was to hand speaks more credibly of deliberation and intent rather than the spontaneity purported by defence counsel.

We have heard the victim describe being held around the throat and stabbed in the head, the neck and the right shoulder. The offender dragged her away from the door and kicked it shut. The deadlock would have therefore made access impossible from the outside. In any event the neighbours heard nothing untoward and, on this occasion, raised no alarm. The victim recalls the offender forcing her to the floor where he sat astride her torso and continued stabbing her. She pleaded with him to stop, to calm down, to which the offender replied, 'I am calm.'

The offender put the knife to his own wrist and sliced it. Mr Russick then proceeded to stab himself in the chest and neck. Again he stabbed the victim in the chest. She begged him not to stab her in the chest, so the offender rolled her over and stabbed her in the back between the shoulder blades.

She screamed, but her screams were stifled by the offender, who pronounced, 'We are Romeo and Juliet. We are meant to be together. We'll die in each other's arms. Don't you understand? Our love will last forever.'

The victim believed that to agree with this notion of a lover's pact was her only chance to allay the assault.

She said, 'Yes. But if we are Romeo and Juliet then shouldn't we share the knife? Shouldn't we go out together?'

Or words to that effect.

After a moment the offender agreed and handed her the knife. They saw that the blade of the knife was broken, the tip of which was later found embedded in the victim's scapula. The offender went into the kitchen to fetch another knife. Meanwhile the victim grabbed her phone and attempted to ring her father. Returning, the offender snatched the phone from her hand and resumed stabbing the victim with a new knife. Again her screams were muted, and she collapsed. The offender then sent several text messages via the victim's phone to her father. These amounted to messages which Mr Gilfoyle believed to be from his daughter. They stated that a reconciliation had taken place between Ms Gilfoyle and Mr Russick, and that she had decided to stay. They were unpacking. She would not need her father's help after all. She would ring and explain it all at a later time.

These messages are recorded in the annexures to this statement.

Outside the house Mr Gilfoyle replied with a message of his own, 'OK.'

Whereupon he left the scene.

By this time the offender had removed his shirt and lain down beside the victim.

The offender said, 'Are you ready to die now?'

The victim said, 'Yes.'

He handed her the second knife in order to expedite the pact. He said he was ready. She then stabbed the offender in the stomach and twisted the knife, to which the offender said, 'Good shot.'

When she withdrew the blade a portion of his intestines extruded from the puncture wound. The victim was nauseous. The offender rolled over and the victim has stated she believes she stabbed him between three and six times in the back. (It would appear, as evidenced by the injuries, to be more.) She also stabbed him in the neck and buttocks, although these injuries were superficial. The victim believed that her only chance of survival was to wait until the offender was weakened by blood loss. To this end she declared that she was ready to lie down and die in his arms, as in the misconstrued narrative of Romeo and Juliet. The offender took the knife and proceeded to stab himself five times in the thigh. He then lay down beside her and she tried to soothe him by stroking his face. At some stage they went into the bedroom and lay down on the double bed. For how long is uncertain. Ms Gilfoyle recalls being thankful that the glassware had not broken during the fracas.

It would seem that they both drifted in and out of consciousness. At one point the victim, confused and debilitated, disengaged herself and tried to crawl towards the door, but the offender awoke and dragged her back into the kitchen. He took her keys and threw them behind the fridge so she could not unlock the door. There were several phone messages which were ignored. There was a bottle of tequila from which they both drank. For a time they both sat on the kitchen floor, drinking and bleeding, in the mistaken belief that this was some form of romantic consummation. Needless to say, as can be seen in the photographs, the place was awash.

In an attempt to keep him talking, the victim asked if the offender remembered a particular scene from Romeo and Juliet? He said that he did, and went to fetch the book so that she could read the passage to him as they died. While he was gone the victim, seizing the moment, fled into the bathroom where she was able to lock the door. She was immediately pursued by the offender. She opened the window and, climbing onto the basin, was able to push out the fly wire screen. The offender meanwhile, shoulder-charged the bathroom door and attempted to kick it down.

Note the photographs of stains (#31 within exhibit A) and damage sustained to this door.

The victim had managed to tumble out the window and drop two metres to the ground. By the time the offender was able to unfasten and emerge from the back door, the victim, covered in blood and still in immediate fear for her life, had staggered around the side of the house into Clyde Street, where a pass-er-by (witness # AG) intervened. The offender, still armed with the (second) knife, pursued the victim across the front yard, but upon seeing the passerby, (witness # AG) halted, no doubt to the extreme relief of those on the footpath. At this point the neighbours did hear screaming. The offender then turned and retreated to the house.

Following this rapid sequence of events witness AG was able to call the emergency services. The time of this call is recorded as 2.38 p.m., so the victim's harrowing ordeal had been going on for several hours. The victim lay down on the nature strip. An ambulance arrived and she was treated at the scene before being removed to hospital where her numerous wounds (amounting to 29 stab wounds and lacerations, one lung punctured in three places, and also two fractured ribs) were cleaned and repaired. The knife blade was removed from her back, (see exhibit D). I note also a fractured clavicle caused as a result of the fall from the bathroom window.

When police entered the house they found the offender unconscious on the floor of the kitchen. They noted the protrusion of some of his intestines which the offender had unsuccessfully tried to push back. He was in a state of near exsanguinity and if it was not for the work of the paramedic team he would not be here today.

A half-empty bottle of tequila stood on the bench. A book lay face down in the blood.

These facts are all beyond reasonable doubt.

I find that the victim, Anna Gilfoyle, conducted herself with intelligence and fortitude under extraordinary circumstances, both terrifying and prolonged. We have heard the effects of this in the submission of the victim impact statement. The physical and psychological scars of which will in all likelihood never leave her.

Stand up, sir.

Taking into account the offender's early guilty plea, also his previous good record and testimonials from significant members of the community as to his upstanding character and his level of education, I formulate the sentence along the following lines. I do not take into consideration the wounds, some self-inflicted, some inflicted by the victim herself, received by the offender in the course of committing these crimes. The fact that the offender himself clearly intended to die during this assault, is also not a mitigating factor. (I duly note for the appropriate service providers this offender's evident propensity for self-harm.) I do take into account the fact that the offender was in recent months assaulted in prison while on remand awaiting trial, and that this assault along with its long term adverse consequences was the inadvertent result of publicity surrounding the case. This should not be calculated as part of the overarching punishment and its determinants. I also take into account the likelihood or otherwise of the prisoner reoffending, and his prospects for rehabilitation which are encouraging. I note his family support.

While not in the worst category of offending these crimes are nevertheless very serious and are treated by this court as such. On the charge of aggravated kidnapping and deprivation of liberty I sentence you to five years imprisonment to commence on 14 February 2014. On the charge of wounding with intent to murder I sentence you to a non-parole term of twelve years, a total sentence aggregate of seventeen years incarceration, to expire on 14 February 2031. You will be eligible for parole from 15 February 2026. Mr Luscombe, do you have anything further to add regarding the matter of sentencing?

Mr Luscombe: No, your Honour.

Ms Francelli, does the prosecution have any other concerns?

Ms. Francelli: No, your Honour.

Then thank you, ladies and gentlemen. Good afternoon.

The Buddy Cell

'Daz.'

His voice again.

'Daz?'

All this wheedling. I don't suppose for a moment that anyone will take it into their hearts to feel sorry for me for this. Or Ron for that matter. I don't suppose many people give us much thought at all anymore. Wheedling is probably the least thing they think I should have to put up with. Not that I'm fishing for sympathy. What would be the point? Sympathy is like poison to me, like a copper coin in a fish tank. Ron is old now. That won't win him any votes in the *nice* stakes. A good old fellow. Good old boy who has done his time. Or most of it. Old enough to fart ash. Can't be too long now. I just wish he'd stop with the whining.

'Daz,' he calls through the open door.

Soon I'll get up and go in and see what he wants, but not yet.

I haven't shaken off the lingering depths of the night. Too busy staring at the grey swirls of paint on the walls. You can almost see what direction the roller was travelling in, like a paddock of wheat leaning with the wind. Nice. Pretty soon the nostalgia fades and it's just paint on a wall going nowhere. Besides, I know what he wants.

The walls provide hours of distraction for the easily distracted. Sometimes I trace a pattern with a finger, but as soon as you blink the pattern disappears. I'd be interested to know, although I appreciate that no one else would be, how much time I have actually spent staring at walls, if you added it all up. Ten years? Longer. Long after the random meaning in the stains has vanished. It's just paint. Just stains. A window over there, facing west, dark or light or sometimes grey. When the light fades there is a light switch and a light switch implies an act of volition. A choice. A vote.

'Daz.'

I vote we turn the light on. Or off. One day Ron will cease to call. I guess, that day, it'll take me a while to work out why the silence is so pure, why it's dragging on so long. I daresay I'll enjoy it, the unaccustomed peace and quiet. Maybe I'll wait a while before I open the buddy door and see him in his bed still as a lump of concrete, or perhaps a lump of dough. It'll depend on the season. I'll delay my pressing of the buzz-up button a little longer. *It must have happened in his sleep,* I'll say, *I never heard a thing.*

'Daz.'

Not this morning though.

'What?'

'It's happened again.'

'Fuck me dead.'

I swing my legs over the edge of the foam mattress. The door between our cells creaks open. Ron standing there on the cold floor, his pyjama pants sopping wet. He hasn't put his teeth in. He looks like a wobbegong out of water.

'Jesus, Ron.'

The hairless skin on his concave chest is loose like a plucked chicken, somewhere between refrigeration and decay; something wrapped half-heartedly in muslin. Look at him. The Human Achievement. Doesn't look as though he could ever have hurt a fly.

Ron is in his seventies now. I suppose I could find out exactly where in his seventies if I was that way inclined. I'm not. Daresay I'll look like that before too long.

'Sorry, Daz.'

'Yeah, sure you are.'

'I'd do the same for you, you know.'

'Can't you put your teeth in for God's sake.'

I reef his pyjama pants down. Look at that. Strange to think how that flaccid little slug could have caused so much trouble in its day. Mine too, if it comes to that. Mind of its own, not that I'm minimizing. No, I own what I did. I toss his saturated duds into a corner and fetch his other pair out of the tub. He stands waiting for me, chicken skin shivering. I hold the clean pair open. He rests a bony hand on my shoulder and lifts one foot. His dick just there. Other foot. I wiggle the strides up to their hitching post, hanging off his hips like a rag off a scarecrow, or the parchment off a dead cow in drought.

'Thanks, Daz.'

'Yeah yeah.'

When he's dressed I rinse out the wet pair in the sink, hang them on the end of his bed. Takes a long time to get any warm water. Can warm water be considered a natural right? During this adventure Ron reaches into his cup and slips his dentures in. The uppers and the lowers do not quite meet so that he usually has trouble biting clean through his crusts. They don't even *clack* like they're supposed to. He has to tear off small mouthfuls and toss them towards the back of his throat. I have first dibs on his cucumber. Funny that a pair of dentures has come back to haunt him like this.

Well, not funny anymore.

A lockdown today, which means we're going to be stuck like this, in here enjoying each other's company all day, *all day,* while they make a token attempt at searching the place. There's been plenty of warning so everyone has had time to get rid of whatever they have to get rid of, whatever is worth searching for. Not that being stuck in here is anything new. And for Ron it makes no diff, really. Can't get down the stairs anymore, so most of the time he's stuck up here on the top landing like a rare plant on top of the fucking mountain. You think it'd be a simple thing to move him to the ground floor so he could hobble out into the sunshine every now and then, but alas. Weekdays I can go to work. So I do. The sunshine, or the rain, in the dash between 4-wing and Industries. And when I come back there's Ron with a wet crotch waiting for me. But not today. Today's a day for staring at the walls, like a crab at the bottom of the sea staring at the sand. After a few years of it you come to realize that boredom is just another thing you have to get used to. You come to realize that anything is bearable.

I keep thinking about the dentures. A plain pair of dentures found under the seat of his Volkswagon all those years ago. Who would have thought? Proved to be exhibit # X, Y, Z—whatever it was—in the Crown's case against him. Physical evidence. He told me, one of our long nights together, how she had taken them out to do the business for a fifty when he clocked her on the head with the wheel brace and forgot to look for them later. Swings and roundabouts I suppose you'd have to call that. Sitting under the passenger seat all that time. That was the first one.

'Thanks, Daz,' he says again, that plastic ivory gleaming wetly in his mouth. Everything else about Ron looks old, apart from the teeth. The Dentist is coming in September to fit him out with a new pair, but in the meantime it's amusing to see him look hungrily at an apple, then slowly shake his head as at a lost cause.

'I'm just about fuckin' sick of this Ron,' I tell him.

'I know. You think I'm having fun?'

'More fun than me.'

'You'll be old one day, then you'll know.'

'I never thought I'd live this bloody long.'

'Me neither,' he says.

'You might wake up dead one day.'

'Mmm.'

I think we're both talking generally here. About life, as they say, meaning life.

'At least you've got someone to change your fuckin' nappy,' I say.

'There'll be someone for you.'

'Someone to stuff a pillow over my face I hope.'

'Don't be like that Daz.'

We do whatever it is we do to pass the moment.

'I suppose they'll force some poor sap in here to help me. Don't like to think that far ahead. You'd think, in a situation like this, you wouldn't have to do any of this shit. That you'd be exempt.'

'I guess not,' says Ron. 'I never gave it any thought.'

I go back to my side of the cave. Pretty soon, there being nowhere else to go, and because it is a privilege being two-out in the buddy cell, Ron hobbles into my half of the slot. We spend our days going back and forth into the stale air of each other's personal space, as if wherever the other is must be more interesting than here. Ron hunches over his walking stick like a question mark.

'Are you gunna stay in bed all day?'

'What else do you want me to do?' I ask, angered by the fact that he cannot see we have this conversation every morning.

'Do you want to play cards?'

'No, I'm sick of cards.'

'Do you want a brew?'

'No.'

'I'll put the jug on.'

He shuffles back to his cell. I can hear him fucking about, filling up his kettle, tipping a bit out. He turns on his telly. Music from the cartoons, just ending. *Stay tuned for the Good Morning Show with . . .*

The music changes. Because of his deafness the *Good Morning Show* blares loudly, '*Good Morning Everybody.*'

Pretty soon he's back in the doorway just standing there like the fucking ghost of Christmas past. I don't look up at him. Then I do.

'You want a brew now?' he asks.

'Yeah. All right. Make sure it's normal.'

To wean him off nicotine the Clinic has given Ron patches, but all he does is stew them up in his cup and drink it like tea. I sit up. I lift my legs. I go into his room and sit on his bed. So far so good. I suppose he's right. They probably will find someone for me when I'm decrepit enough, just as I've been conscripted for this job. Trouble is I don't feel that debilitated just yet. Mostly I still feel like a young bloke. Like I did when I first come in. Which is to say something like immature, like something on the prowl, ready for mischief. I can feel it fading though, the anti-social tendency; the rebel. Hot blood cooling. I'll be fifty-nine next birthday. Quite the conservative.

I was a young man when I first come inside and time stopped. People must still think I look like those old photos the papers trot out every now and then. Anniversary of the death and so on. Why should I grow up and face the consequence of my actions, when my thoughts are stuck back there at the worst moment, or the worst they know about, the *nadir* (a shrink's word) by which I am judged. Ron too. We don't talk too much about the past. Apart from when I need to put him in his place. Then I remind him about the teeth under the car seat and he tells me to shut the fuck up and I tell him to make me and he asks how many fingers I've got in my pockets, do I need a few extra ones to add up my IQ? I bristle. This is a barbed reference to the (alleged) fingers missing from Tracey Collet's left hand that the papers maintain—they always *maintain*—were 'found to be missing'. Found to be missing, it's almost enough to make you laugh. Well, I tell Ron, as I told the court at the time what would I want with Tracey Collet's fingers? And furtherfuckingmore Tracey Collet was alive, breathing unassisted, when I left the room which is more than you'll be if I take that walking stick and give you a pounding with it.

We probably have a few hours of silence after this conversation, and all the others like it. The door is shut but not locked. Soon enough we both cool down. We're buddies.

At least, I tell him when the air has cleared, my record doesn't list the historical conviction of failing to vote.

'Never voted in my life,' he says, proud of himself. 'They only caught me once.'

'I'd like to vote,' I say, nostalgically.

'Why?'

'It's just another thing they've taken away.'

Ron laughs.

'Better off out of it,' he says.

We have reached our status quo, our *nadir*. You get used to it. The fingers in my pocket, the teeth in his car, failing to vote. We each know where the other stands. There's no point comparing headlines.

We finish our tea. I rinse the mugs. I sit beside him on the bed. He asks me to scratch his back where he can no longer reach.

'Might have a shower today,' he says.

'You better.'

The advertisements on the telly are interesting. They give you a window into what the world is like on the outside. What we are missing. We have strong opinions on the worth and efficacy of certain consumer items, potato peelers and so on. *Never peel a potato again*, says the spruiker. Sometimes the view out that window is a painful one.

'Oh no,' Ron says, 'Sorry Daz, I've done it again. That tea's gone straight though me.'

'For fuck's sake, the shit hole's just there. Can't you hobble that far?'

'Sorry mate.'

'You haven't got anymore pants.'

'Can I borrow a pair of yours?'

'No.'

'Well, are the others dry?'

I feel the pyjama pants at the end of the bed.

'Not yet.'

'I suppose they'll have to do.'

'Give me a moment.'

I think this must be what it's like for new parents, not that I would know, but at least they can look forward to growing out of it. I watch the telly. How to make an ikebana arrangement with cuttings from your own backyard. That's interesting.

'You want to watch something else?' he asks.

'I vote we watch this.'

I can smell Ron sitting next to me on his bed. I let him stew in it. I'll have to change the sheets too, which is why I never let him sit on my cot. He sucks at the loose teeth in his mouth. They make him look too happy. Sometimes you'd like to wipe the smile right off his face. I go back to my cell, about half a dozen paces—he was alive when I left the room, breathing unassisted. Nothing has changed in here. I open the window to air the place. To close it again will be an act of volition. I lie on the bed. The wall just there. Wheat leaning with the wind.

'Daz.'

'Wait.'

The fingers in my pocket (they're not there, but they're real) dragging me down, dragging me down to the cold depths of myself.

Young Men and the Sea

Shane and Chook had been smoking a lot before they got the idea of skipping Sydney and sailing north. They used to do everything together in those days, so why not this? They took four cases of Doctor Tooheys and half a pound of hydro from the stash they had not paid Billy Abdullah for. They had to leave urgently. They pinched a dinghy from the Rose Bay Yacht Club wharf and rowed clumsily about the dark waters of the marina. They choked on their laughter when they bumped into other empty boats. There was no security guard anywhere. Music drifted from one large yacht moored to the main pier, but they steered clear of that and no one came.

They selected a boat, tied to its buoy, without much discretion other than its air of abandonment. It was called *Bella Rosa III* and looked like it might go fast. They climbed on board and ferreted about in the cabins below. There was a wardrobe full of some woman's clothes. A few photographs in frames. Apart from hotwiring, Shane had completed a year of a mechanic's apprenticeship and so knew about engines. He got the motor started while Chook cut through the moorings at the hawsehole. Not a light came on as they chugged slowly onto the midnight harbour. No ferries ran. No pleasurecraft. No visiting naval vessels. They ignored the great arc of lights that was the bridge hanging between its stone pylons, a red light winking at the top. They hung a right—No, Chook said to himself, get it right sailor, they veered to *starboard*. The lights of the north shore flats shining to? to port (bugger it, shining on the *left*) and to the right New South Head Road winding its way through Vaucluse, Bellevue Hill, Watson's Bay, wankers all of 'em.

They had polished off two cans before they reached the heads, and Chook spewed them right back up once they passed the lights of Manly towards the open sea. They found seasick tablets in a cabinet below and took about eight each. It was still all good fun, and the adrenalin and adventure of a fancy yacht with cupboards full of food and a swishy sound system kept them amused for hours. A pity there was no decent music to listen to. They could see no stars, but being city boys, neither of them could much see the point of stars.

Shane only remembered how to hoist a mizzen, so they kept on chugging out to sea under the motor. After all, all they had to do was turn left (all right, *port*) and head north. But once the lights of the city disappeared behind them, there was no landmark to tell them where exactly to turn. They smoked. They drank. They slept a little. In the morning they were shaken awake by the rolling of the boat—a fire extinguisher had been loosed from its clasp—and saw they were heading towards the sun in the northern sky.

The weather clouded over and the ocean grew choppier. Shane knew enough not to let the boat turn side on into the swell and so steered the yacht nose first (or was it prow?) up and down and over the waves. Chook had to go below decks to mull up, because the spray bursting over the side kept wetting the papers. He liked using nautical phrases like that: below decks; weigh anchor; shiver me timbers. When were the flying fish going to start landing on the deck? He remembered Coral Island and Treasure Island. All those islands. His can of beer kept sliding across the tilting table like something from Gilligan's Island. Green about the gills as he felt, he cooked up some beans he found in the yacht's fancy kitchen, what was it called? the galley, yeah.

'Do you want some fang?' he called up to Shane.

'What is it?'

'Beans, we got lots of beans.'

'Fuck no,' came the windswept reply, 'get us another can.'

For two days, three days, they dealt with the waves, which continued to grow. When were they going to hit some calm water? Chook was sick of feeling sick. The doldrums, that's what he wanted a bit of, where were they? They didn't even know what they were going to do when they got to New Guinea; they fantasized about sitting on beaches; picking coconuts. Anything they liked. People smuggling, there might be a quid in that. Plans going up in smoke.

At the end of the week they had emptied the larder (fuck what its proper name was) and finished most of the beer. Finished the cognac too, found in the bar downstairs. Still the seas were growing taller. Chook had grown used to the rush of the yacht riding up the side of one wall of water, broaching the foamy peak, and sliding down the valley between the next two waves.

Shane said, 'Man, we're gunna run out of petrol at this rate.'

'Where do you reckon we are?' Chook asked.

'Must be past Brisbane by now. Maybe Fraser Island. Or even Mackay.'

'You don't know where the fuck we are.'

'Yes I do. We're heading north.'

'Can't we put up some sails?'

'Sails will tip us right over Chook. Listen to that wind. Anyway, I can't remember the knots.'

'Then can't we just turn around and go back? I'm sick of this shit.'

'You want me to radio Billy Abdullah and tell him we're coming?'

Spray stung their faces. Or was it rain? They couldn't tell. The gale, for that is what the weather had become, flicked them from the crest of one wave to the next. Chook wished the boat would hide for a bit down in the gullies between the raging waters. The mizzen at the rear tore loose and flapped crazily like a flag for a moment before disappearing altogether into the darkness. Hours passed and only the greyness of the sky full of rain told them it was not night.

When Chook was at the wheel Shane came on deck with a plastic box he had found.

'What's that?'

'Flares.'

'What for?'

'Just in case. You better put this on too.'

Shane handed Chook a yellow life jacket. Why the fuck hadn't they been wearing these all along? A wave crashed over the side and flooded the decks to the knee. The noise of it receding sucked all their words out too.

Finally Shane said, 'I think I've sussed how the radio works.'

'What for? Some easy-listening music.'

'In case we have to call for help, fool.'

'This ain't like stealing a car you know. This is a million dollar yacht. If we tell them where we are we'll get ten years for this.'

'You might, with your record.'

The mast above them rocked like a metronome. Shane staggered below. The blackness of the sky was inseparable from the blackness of the water. Upness and downness also, inseparable. Air and water, also. Chook thought about all the romantic crap he had heard about the sea. About those books his old cell mate had made him read. Or read to him. Lord fucking Jim. Moby fucking Dick. The old man and the fucking sea. It was all right for him, at least the old man had had good weather.

On the tenth day the petrol ran out. They did not hear the motor sputter and die, but they felt the vibrations they had grown used to beneath their feet suddenly cease. It was like their hearts stopping. Almost immediately a wave knocked the boat side on and the only thing preventing Chook from being swept overboard was the wheel he was clinging to, which wrenched the rudder about. The boat righted itself. Slid down the next wave's shattering face. Wave? It was more like a cliff. At the base they felt their guts might fall out. They rode up the other side, fearing the peak like the Big Dipper at Luna Park, front on once more.

Chook went down the ladder. All the dope was drenched, but he was hoping Shane might have had the foresight to stash a little bit of dry stuff away for himself. Everything was drenched. Chook hadn't been dry for over a week. He clung to the doorway. Shane was at the radio.

'No I don't know the global positioning code,' he was saying, 'That's right, Bella Rosa III.'

There was a pause, then static.

He turned to Chook.

'What did you leave the wheel for?'

'What's the fuckin' difference? We haven't got any power. We're in angel gear. Who're you talkin' to?'

'Coastguard.'

'Have you given us up?'

Shane had to gather his words. 'They say that when we sink to give off a final mayday, then get in the life boat and fire off a flare every fifteen minutes.'

'*When* we sink?'

'Yeah.'

'Where is the fuckin' life boat?'

'Down the stern . . . I haven't got a watch.'

'Me neither.'

The yacht rolled and bucked. Empty cans skittered about the floor. The cabin lights went out.

'Which coastguard was it?'

'Dargaville. New Zealand. They heard about us.'

'No shit. New Zealand?'

Water was spitting into the cabin. It had the greyness of day-light about it.

'Yeah . . . Chook, I don't reckon we planned this too well.'

'No. They're gunna laugh at us in six-wing.'

Neither of them laughed. A wave tipped the boat almost to right angles, Shane held up in the air by the fixed table. It took a long time to right itself. They clung to the sides of the table, as the solid world about them plummeted and rolled, not avoiding, but not catching each other's eye.

The Phone Rings

'Hello?'
'Hello, Mr Tran.'
'Yes.'
'It's Dwayne calling from the Royal Society for the preservation of— '

'Hello?'
'Hello, Mr Tran?'
'Yes.'
'Sorry to interrupt your afternoon, I'm calling from the Heritage Institute of— '

'Hello, Mr Tran.'
'No. Can I take a message?'
'Is Mr Tran available?'

'No. I am his wife.'

'This is a courtesy call, but we were wondering if you had considered making a donation to—'

Mr Tran stretches and yawns so widely that his jaw cracks. He makes a single note on his notepad. The guard comes and motions for him to go. It is time for lunch.

If I said that I had a record of all the phone calls you had made in the last, say, three years—how many of them would be cold calls from charities? I pick this category at random. Alternatively, how many would be wrong numbers? Crank calls? How many ordinary domestic queries for persons not home at the moment? How many casual conversations? Other children calling your children. More wrong numbers. Messages left after the beep. Dial tones. Engaged signals. Political canvassers. The list could go on. How many?

Calls coming in and calls going out. Let's not forget those. Who are these people you call? Plumbers perhaps; motor mechanics occasionally. Refrigerator repairmen when required, other handymen and women. Friends, colleagues. Who are these people Mr Tran talks to? Takeaway food orders, account enquiries, government departments, babysitters, wrong numbers, pay-by-phone bills, mother on Mothers Day, spouse's work number, messages left after the beep, dental appointments, even the emergency services, if needs be, in an emergency. How many might this amount to? I guess quite a lot.

And amongst these phone calls over—say—three years, two or three which constitute enough evidence to secure your guilt, conviction and sentencing to fourteen years hard labour for conspiring to import a commercial quantity of prohibited goods.

Mr Tran has just this problem.

The phone rings.

'Hello, Mr Tran?'

'Yes.'

'It's Bob O'Toole from Strathfield Motors. Your car is ready to be picked up. We've had to replace the muffler, so with parts and labour the bill will come to—'

Hang on. Go back. Conspiring to what? Mr Tran is understandably astonished.

Which phone calls, his nice lawyer asks on his behalf, would these be?

Why the ones which substantiate your client's guilt.

But which ones specifically, asks the lawyer, can we hear them? Why?

Because we don't believe such evidence exists. How do we know if it's his voice on the tape?

The judge believes it to be so.

My client would like to hear for himself in order that appeal proceedings can be instigated so as to refute this scurrilous allegation. It is not him on the tape.

This might have been better brought up at trial.

Er, circumstances beyond our control etcetera.

This is a piscatorial exercise, however, since the Crown is not in the business of withholding evidence we are prepared to release all the recordings in our possession.

Including the particular pertaining to the current matter?

Of course.

Thank you.

The onus shall then be on your client—Mr Tran—to show why the content of such phone calls does not demonstrate culpability.

(Mr Tran, slouching in the corner of the dock, responds to the sound of his name.) Huh?

Tell us which phone calls you doubt?

Which phone calls?

That is for you to tell us.

I no understand.

Hardly our problem, Mr Tran.

Mr Tran worries the sandpaper of his whiskers. His nice lawyer, Mr Luscombe, shuffling papers into his briefcase, worries about nothing.

Four thousand.

That is how many phone calls Mr Tran has to examine. All presented on a series of compact disks, which he listens to through a pair of padded silver ear muffs, like a pilot at the controls of a doomed recording studio.

The phone rings.

'Good evening, Mr Tran?'

'No, he's not here.'

'Who am I speaking to?'

'My name is Mrs Tran. Can I take a message?'

'I'll call back later.'

He is living his life over again, listening to his own conversations. And those of others. Here they are: ephemeral fragments of the past, frozen, numbered, digitalised. He listens intently, like a monk to his own breathing. His own squeaky voice—does he really sound like that? His wife Ang Soo's voice. A hundred other voices. Some he recognises. Friends, colleagues. Many are just strangers' voices, selling things, asking for information or donations; wheedling, demanding, wanting his opinion, his time, his money. Whether he pledged his money or not, what does it matter now? These are conversations from which the significance has atrophied. They come to him like the light from a dead star. Does he wonder, if he could see himself, is there any meaning to be gleaned from listening to such pointless, dead dialogue? It is proof, he hopes, that he once existed. He eavesdrops on conversations his children have with their friends; his wife with her sisters; himself with his market pals. No insight there. He does not know the names of his children's friends. It is like scratching the dust from the archives and shrouds of a vaguely familiar people. He did not know, for instance that his son, a mere boy, was in possession of so much money. Money he had scrimped and saved. Or what particular brand of audio technology he was saving for. He did not know, for instance, that his daughter had been in love. Is she still? He is desperate to know. The sound of her voice pierces him.

The phone rings.
    'Hello, Mr Tran.'
    'Yes.'

'I'm from the Lions Club, it's our annual ring around. We're trying to raise funds, and I wondered if you'd like to buy some raffle tickets. First prize is—'

Is this what they mean? Is this the evidence of conspiracy? The conversations are so banal that, after many months trapped in the past, he finds himself falling asleep at the desk.

Then one day . . .

The phone rings.

'Yes.'

'Is Tran there?'

'No, he's out.'

'I need to see you.'

'I told you never to call here.'

A man's voice. His wife's, Ang Soo, and the unfamiliar voice of a man. Then . . .

'Hello Ang Soo.'

'Kai Cho, I told you not to call here.'

'I need to see you.'

'No. I cannot. It is not right. I am married.'

'I must.'

A pause. Her breath.

'All right.'

Mr Tran's face falls. Suddenly he is wide awake. He replays the call. He flings the headphones from him with an angry gesture and thumps the desk. No, he doesn't. He remains stoic and immutable as a statue. Who is Kai Cho? The intent behind his words says more than the words themselves. He has not been listening carefully enough. He'll have to start again. They are speaking in code.

He realises, even though he was fully involved in living it, that he has only occupied a small portion of his life. His life is a small pond that he has never seen to the bottom of. Who is Kai Cho? Certainly not the accessory they named in court as accomplice to the ringleader—*Yes, you Mr Tran.*

In fact, so far, there are no phone calls incriminating him at all. He sounds alarmingly normal. He sounds like every other Asian man to an Australian jury. There is nothing but the roaring dinosaur of his past confronted by the sudden, cold shock of his surroundings.

Every morning, after muster, he comes to the gaol library. He sharpens his pencil into the cup of his hand and puts the shavings in the bin, then he puts on his pilot's headphones and presses the button. The phone rings. His past comes alive, gnawing at him. I can only imagine what he might be listening to. When I ask him he says there are 2724 phone calls to go. But, he worries, what if he hasn't been listening properly? Time is running out. Who is Kai Cho? Has he heard the voice before? Every day he listens, no longer for the coded messages of costings and drop-offs that the prosecution alleges; not for rendezvous points, nor the names of the co-accused that he knows will keep him locked away. If he hears them. If they exist. What do they say? He is not so sure they do exist. By the same token, he is not so sure they do not. He is losing his grip. Just what do they know? What does he know of himself? He chews his pencil. He, with the benefit of hindsight is learning too much about his life. Namely that he has a vast capacity for ignorance. He knows nothing. What did happen in the past? He is becoming more like an animal regulated by reflex, responding to the ringing of bells. A guard comes and growls at him—he's wanted at the clinic—but he does not understand the command. No English. The ominous years ahead are shedding their meaning like a snake's skin. A small pond evaporating. Each day he comes to listen, in patient agony, still and focused as a shard of glass, waiting for Ang Soo to answer the phone a long time ago.

Reading with Daddy

When Katie's father went to gaol for dropping a rock from an overpass, causing a truck to swerve and hit the buttress of a bridge, it took Katie a long time to reconcile herself to his absence. What a fool he was. That behaviour was the reckless act of a delinquent schoolboy, not someone old enough to know better. Katie was not privy to the details of these adult condemnations; his foolishness, whether or not the truck driver lived, how many years he got. She only knew that her father had stopped coming. A big, ill-defined hole had opened up that she could not see the edges of. How deep was it? Was there anything at the bottom? Her schooling began to suffer. You could see her ever so slowly giving up. I couldn't bring myself to tell her how much better off she was. Genes were all very well, but foolishness as a role model was something she could do without. She kept a photo of him by her bed, and in those tired, teary moments before dropping off to sleep she might sometimes say, 'My daddy has beautiful eyes,' before hugging me harder than she needed to.

I must admit that I was long over Steve's post-adolescent antics by then. When we split-up I saw his personality regressing, more and more seeking solace in the moment. The maturity and confidence fatherhood had given him began to peel away like the shell of a boiled egg. He started drinking again, behaving like a teenaged goose in a middle-aged body, so that by the time Katie was six or seven I had had enough. A piece of string is only so long. When I left I didn't leave with much. I started from scratch but what I started with he had no claim to. I was getting myself back together. And yet I did want Steve to have a relationship with Katie. Or rather, the reverse. I wanted Katie to grow up knowing that her father was not a figment of her imagination. He was real and also flawed. There was a lesson there somewhere. So I encouraged his phone calls; his sporadic visits where he'd take her to the park or the plaza or, once, to eat fish and chips by the beach. I did not let him know how grateful I was for the reprieve, for perhaps I wasn't grateful, perhaps I resented the fact that he wasn't there all the time to give me a rest when I was tired. To give me back a few moments of my own. The part of me that hated him I set aside for Katie's sake.

And then he went to gaol. And Katie now wonders where her father with his beautiful eyes has disappeared to. And I am implicit in covering up for him. I want to keep this precarious balance because it is the only equilibrium I have. I couldn't, and can't, bring myself to tell her to forget about him. Imagine the issues she'd have with me in twenty years time if I did that? We've already been through the *Why did you drive him away?* questions, the scenarios where nothing I say can possibly be right. I supposed that one day I would have to explain to her where he had got to, why he no longer visited. But not yet. Plenty of time for the truth.

Then, out of the blue a parcel arrived. On the back of it was printed the address of the prison, also a lavender stamp announcing *APPROVED*. Inside was a book. Beatrix Potter. Also, wrapped in bubble wrap, a CD.

'It's from Daddy.'

I sounded more excited than I felt. We sat on the couch and I pressed *play*. Steve's voice came from the speakers.

'It is said that the effect of eating too much lettuce is soporific . . . '

Katie did not seem too fussed about the meaning of soporific. I understand that language comes before conceptual dawning, so that the ache of missing him, I hoped, was less keen without the words to define it. This is what I told myself, anyway. Wishful thinking. She was simply amazed in a lip-quivering fashion, and then delighted to hear her father's voice mumbling away. It was a lovely moment to witness. We turned the pages together, following the story. Sometimes in the background of the recording you could hear bells, or a muffled PA announcement, or doors slamming, but they were only in the background. I have to say Steve was no Jack Thompson in terms of his narrative style. Peter Rabbit spoke in exactly the same monotone as Mr McGregor. If anything his voice was pretty soporific itself, but try telling that to Katie. She didn't care. It was her daddy's voice speaking to her. Reading a story to *her*. Something he had never taken the time to do before. She followed every word as if it verified her existence.

When it was over his voice said, 'Well Katie, that's the end. I hope you liked the story. Bye.'

Katie must have listened to that CD twenty times without moving from the couch. She was smitten with it. She slept with the book under her pillow. The next day after school she took the CD over the road to Mrs Watson, an elderly widow who knew everything about the neighbourhood, who spent a lot of time in her garden. Of course she was elderly to Katie, less so for me. Once Katie got over her initial fear of the aged face she found Mrs Watson friendly enough, she said, like a dog you know won't bite, who likes his tummy scratched.

'She was so proud of her daddy,' Mrs Watson told me later, bailed up at the letterbox one sun-bright afternoon, the patch-work nature strips all around. 'It breaks your heart, doesn't it?'

I didn't know what to say to that, a fresh salvo of bills in my hand. Mrs Watson glanced at my decrepit front yard and in that instant, perhaps I saw it in her face, or else with my own eyes, that it was something I somehow deserved.

About a month later another parcel arrived. It had Katie's name on it. I placed it on the kitchen table and the wet clothes basket on the floor. I went outside to unpeg the dry washing from the line. Thank goodness for a sunny afternoon. In a while I heard a squeal and Katie came flying out the back door.

'Look what Daddy sent me.'

She was bouncing on her toes.

'That's nice. Where's the disc?'

'What disc?' Then, 'Ahh,' as she realised what was missing.

She had torn the envelope to shreds looking for it by the time I came back inside. Luckily it had only fallen from the parcel into the clothes basket. No damage. Together, in our differing moods, we sat down with our hot chocolates and listened to Steve intone, 'Once upon a time there was a village shop. The name over the windows was Ginger and Pickles . . . '

It was odd for me to imagine Steve with his missing front tooth and his tattoos saying, 'Once upon a time there was a village shop . . . '

Katie loved it. For me the novelty lasted about half an hour, but Katie played that story over and over. She fetched her photo of him so she could have the image in conjunction with the voice saying the words of Ginger and Pickles. Then, while I was washing the dishes, she ran to her room, slammed the door and burst into tears. When I went in to her she sobbed and sobbed, her pillow quite damp, as if this was the last day of sobbing allowed.

'Why does Daddy have to do bad things?'

'Oh darling, what do you mean?'

'He's in gaol, isn't he?' she wailed.

'What makes you say that?'

There was nothing I could claim as a distraction.

'Mrs Watson told me.'

'Mrs Watson?' (That sour old bitch.)

'Yes. And it's written on the back of Daddy's parcel.'

'You could read that?'

'Yes.'

I glanced out the window and said, 'Look what that silly bird's doing,' but she did not look.

So I had to come clean and tell her. It wasn't quite what I had in mind, but at least now I would no longer have to pretend he was at work—where was he again? On an oil rig? In a mine somewhere? Overseas helping poor people? At last I could put those lies behind me. However, it did make me glare daggers at the old bag across the road, especially when we were both reversing out of our driveways at the same time. She could wait.

The books arrived pretty regularly after that. We went through all of Beatrix Potter. Then Dr Seuss, which took me back like an echo in my blood. Then *Wind in the Willows*, *Blinky Bill*; plenty of others. Quack quack, said the little duck. She was a little bit old for that. Some of them were too young for her. Didn't Steve realise how quickly she was growing up?

'Does he think I'm a baby?'

Nevertheless, Katie learned them off by heart. She began to spout gibberish, like some of the people in the books, as if it was real conversation. I couldn't keep up with her.

One day when I was picking her up after school her teacher spotted me across the asphalt netball court and scurried over.

'Mrs Dormond?'

I turned to her.

'It's Beggs actually. Dormond is Katie's name.'

'Sorry. I'm Vanessa Lyle, Katie's teacher.'

'Yes, I remember.'

'How are you?'

'Fine.'

'Look, to cut straight to the chase. I was just wondering what's been happening at home?'

'What do you mean?' I asked, immediately paranoid. What had I neglected now? 'Nothing.'

'No. I mean in a good way. Something's happened because Katie's reading has gone through the roof.'

'Really?'

'She's top of the class by a mile. And it's been quite sudden. The other day she said she was feeling soporific and wanted to have a rest.'

I laughed at that, and saw that Vanessa—I couldn't bring myself to call someone younger than me Mrs—wasn't having a go, an attitude that was probably my default position. She was genuinely curious. Celebratory, even.

'Her father's been reading to her,' I explained.

It was her turn to say, 'Really?'

Her look said she knew very well where Katie's father was and what he'd done.

I sighed.

'He sends recordings of the books.'

'Well,' she said, 'you can tell him that it's working.'

'Oh we're not—'

'I was wondering if Katie might consider bringing them to school for the class to listen to.'

I was taken aback at this.

'Oh I don't think so. They're so private. I'd have to think about that.'

'Of course, of course. Just an idea,' then she interrupted herself. 'The bus! Sorry, I have to supervise the bus . . . I'll ring you.'

She turned and marched off to her duty, her voice on the wind making the children in the distance sit up and take notice and get back into line.

When we got home Katie raced off, 'Going reading with Daddy,' as she called it. I checked the messages and there was one from some welfare worker at the gaol. I dialled the return number and was soon talking to a woman called—oh I forget what she was called, because with almost clinical sympathy she explained that Steven had been badly bashed. I was stunned.

'How is he?' I asked, or thought I asked.

She must have misheard me to have said merely, 'How?' for she answered, 'With a baked bean can.'

It sounded absurd. Through the window Mrs Watson was out raking her lawn.

'A can of baked beans?'

'Yes. In a sock. It's one of their preferred weapons. A can like that can do a lot of damage.'

'Isn't he in protective custody?'

'It was a protection inmate who assaulted him.'

'Oh God. Is he all right?'

'Well he's in hospital at the moment. Under guard.'

'Will he be all right?' I demanded.

'He has a fractured skull. And I'm afraid it looks like he's going to lose an eye.'

'My God,' I said again. 'What happened?'

'We don't know. The assailant has been charged with grievous bodily harm.'

'No, I mean what was it over?'

'We don't know that either. It may as well have been over nothing. It doesn't take much.'

Mrs Watson was examining her lawn rakings.

'Will he live?'

'Yes. It's not life threatening.'

The phone felt warm and greasy in my hand.

'His eye, you said.'

'Yes, it looks very bad.'

'Will he need a—what's it called?—a prosthesis?'

'I understand it's still too early to tell. However, knowing this department, that won't be their priority.'

'Oh Jesus. Is there anything I can do?'

'He did name you as next of kin.'

'He has a mother in Campsie.'

'Yes. But it's your name on the form.'

'We're not together anymore.'

'I understand that Mrs Dormond—'

'Beggs.'

'Beggs. Sorry. He was asking if it might be possible for you to visit. That is, if you could bring Katie—that is the name of the child?'

'Yes.'

'If you could bring Katie to visit.'

'I see.'

'Sorry to be the bearer of bad news, Mrs Beggs.'

'That's all right,' I said, and our conversation dwindled to its polite termination.

Jesus, I thought. What damage could a can of baked beans in a sock do? I did not mean for it to sound so trite. I felt sick to imagine it. What could I tell Katie? Nothing? She did not need to know. Plenty of time for the truth. I went and stood by her bedroom door and listened to Steve's slow, plodding voice, 'Tom Kitten was very fat, and he had grown; several buttons burst off . . . '

Winter suddenly seemed a step closer.

I busied myself preparing dinner. Rissoles and sweet corn, which were her favourite. For how much longer did I think I could protect her? I wondered. Why, forever, blind as that might be.

I heard the muffled, pedestrian finale.

'Well Katie, that's the end of the story. I hope you liked it. Bye.'

Couldn't he say that he loved her for God's sake? Was that too much trouble? But then he never said that he had loved me. Stop it, I chastised myself, just stop. I felt sick. The stories were his way of saying he loved her. What an accomplishment, in that world of deprivation. Soon she came to the table and we ate heartily, picking skins of corn from between our teeth, right up until the moment Katie asked, 'Mum?'

'Yes darling.'

'What's a prosthesis?'

PART THREE

Dental Tourism

1

After their dinner Susan plonks down three bowls full of ice cream on the table. Nathan tucks in. He has chocolate milk powder sprinkled over his. It gets into his airways and makes him cough. Susan has a moderate portion, but Donald is given a papa bear sized bowl full to the brim. He stares at it. There is distaste and, frankly, fear in his look. He takes up a spoon and reluctantly lifts a tiny amount to his lips, breaching those frontline ramparts. They know what's coming. He knows he doesn't have to eat it, yet his mouth opens. The tip of the spoon goes in. He anticipates, with dread, the electric *zing*, as somewhere in there, his teeth betray their ruined citadel.

In the dead of night he wakes and his face starts throbbing. He knows what has woken him. It is the soft tapping of the dog's tail on the wooden floor as it wags in its sleep. The trouble is the dog is sleeping at the far end of the house, dreaming of rabbits, or whatever dogs dream about. *Tap tap tap.* So faint is Donald's sleep that the muted tap of a dog's tail on the floorboards is enough to wake him. His eyelids roll up like Venetian blinds. It should be made clear that Donald Watkins wakes from faint, tenuous sleep and his face starts throbbing—again. Just lately it's a nightly occurrence. He shouldn't have had that ice cream. Donald is in perpetual discomfort. In his weaker moments he might be tempted to say he is in constant pain.

He moves his head through forty-five degrees and sees the sleeping range of hills that is his wife beneath the blankets beside him. His face throbs. Pulses. He pulls the blanket back, swings his legs over the edge of the bed and sits up. The edge of the window curtain admits some faint street light from outside. Hours to go before dawn. His jaw spasms once, then settles to its steady rhythm. *Fulgurated,* that is a word he has read recently, describing pain, which seems to be so much the worse during the night. Perhaps he can use it as an accurate descriptor with his dentist this afternoon. Just to be precise. He stands up and walks gingerly into the ensuite. Turns on the little night light. Susan's make-up remover and bottles of shampoo clutter the shelf above the basin. The print on the labels is so incredibly tiny he doesn't know who would have eyes good enough to read it. Donald looks at himself in the mirror. His hair sticking up. Lack of proper sleep has pulled the bags under his eyes into a bloodhound's frown. He turns on the tap and splashes water on his face. Throb.

'I can't go on like this,' he says to his reflection.

In the bed behind him Susan rolls over and says, 'Mmm?' reaching her sleeping arm out to his empty side of the bed.

He dares not yawn. In the quiet of the predawn darkness he hears the soft tapping of the dog's tail all the way from the far end of the hall. How can the dog be so happy even as it sleeps? A part of him wants to rudely wake it, remind it of its station in life, but that is a small and spiteful part. He is really a bigger person than that, with empathy for all the smaller creatures in his world. There is a dead fly on the window sill and with a puff of breath he blows it onto the floor.

A couple of Panadeine Forte later with his stewed fruit and he is flying. Not exactly flying, but comparatively, figuratively. He doesn't care that they'll make him constipated. His face now feels happily numb. He'll be able to shave. Pain and shaving don't normally go hand in hand, but these days . . . People don't appreciate what a luxury it is to be pain-free. The ache in his teeth and jaw has abated enough for him to risk a piece of toast, the heat of a cup of tea. Normally that would have had him wincing. As the morning outside creeps into the back yard, where the dog sniffs its way around its landmarks, Donald considers the banality of his days. He hates how he has come to accept this pussyfooting around each moment of pain. How he has to punctuate each day between moments of regulated pill-taking. He wishes for a time when he can again take everything for granted, the way the dog takes for granted that he will open the back door and readmit it to the kitchen.

'How did you sleep, Don?' Susan asks, once the community of the household has roused itself. In her fluffy dressing gown, a cup of tea in her hand, her sleepy allure looks like an advertisement for dressing gowns. Even when she kisses him it aches.

'Terrible.'

'Me too.'

'I don't think I can go on like this,' says Donald.

'Is your mouth hurting again?'

'My mouth hurts always.'

'Poor darling.'

She makes as if to pat his cheek.

'Don't touch me.'

'Have a Panadeine Forte.'

'I've had three.'

'Three! You'll wind up constipated.'

He pops the last corner of toast into his mouth and crunches it. No pain. It's worth it.

'I can completely understand why people get addicted to those things,' he says, standing up, brushing crumbs off his shirt. The radio news itemises a litany of crises, coups and revolutions, to which they pay no attention. There are the more immediate concerns of getting out the door, of getting the day started. Susan will be late home from a meeting and Nathan has an indoor soccer game. And dinner?

'I'm seriously thinking about Bill's suggestion.'

'Bill who?'

'Bill Middleton. From Human Resources.'

'What, that business about Thailand?'

'Yes.'

'Well that sounds desperate.'

'Susan, I am desperate.'

'I'm not going to Thailand.' She flushes her cup under the tap with authority, then places it in the dishwasher.

'I didn't ask you to.'

'I've got too much on.'

'I know.'

'There's the dog.'

'Yes.'

'And there's Nathan.'

'I know,' Donald says again, his cheeks hot. 'I'm not asking you.'

'Aren't you seeing Purcell this afternoon?'

'Yes.'

'See what he's got to say.'

'I know what he'll say. He won't be able to fit me in for six months, then he'll charge an arm and a leg, which I won't be able to afford.'

Susan crosses her arms. Just then, preceded by his size eleven footsteps, Nathan, their son, a big hulking thirteen-year-old comes into the kitchen. Still very much a boy, he lumbers up to his mother and gives her an unselfconscious hug as if he is trying to shake a kitten out of a tree.

'Ouch. Don't squash me.'

'Hi Mum.'

'Morning beautiful.'

Yawning broadly Nathan turns to his father, but Donald holds up his arms protectively.

'Don't touch me.'

Nathan recoils, turning back to Susan. He still smells of sleep. His pyjama buttons are done up in the wrong holes.

'It's all right darling. He's got the grumps again.'

'I have not got the grumps,' says Donald grumpily.

He picks up his briefcase, symbol of his enslavement, and, after their goodbyes, steps through the front door. The banality of his morning follows him out to the garage, and into the car, and the street, and the suburb beyond, stretching all the way into the bright, waking city, like the dog left behind wagging its tail in the new day's heat, taking everything for granted.

2

'The land of smiles,' says Bill Middleton, from Human Resources, flashing Donald a flawless, cheesy grin. His teeth are like Halogen lights.

'How did you get on to them, Bill?'

'Just looked them up.'

Bill pushes the plunger of the coffee pot down into its hot, swirling mire.

'And what did you have done?'

'The works. Fifteen crowns, plus some root canal. My teeth were a right mess. They looked like poppy-seed cake. I have a photo somewhere. Would have cost close to forty grand here. But I did the maths and it only came to seven and a half over there. So you can get fixed up, have a bit of a holiday, lie around on the beach for a few weeks, and still come out ahead. Dental tourism, they call it. Bloody good deal, I say. Can't go past it.'

'I've never been to Thailand.'

'Beautiful people,' says Bill, 'and fabulous dentists. The land of smiles, as I said. You never met a friendlier bunch of characters. Very accommodating.'

'I like Thai food,' says Donald, not wanting to think in stereotypes. The Panadeine Forte are wearing off.

'Then you're home and hosed. Milk?'

'Thanks.'

Bill pours the coffee and adds a dash of milk from the communal bottle in the fridge. His new grin is certainly an enviable asset. It is an achievement. Donald can see Bill is more popular around the office. He's more confident. The boss likes him. He examines the before and after shots Bill carries in his wallet and there is certainly a significant difference. The 'before' shots looked like the teeth of a methylated spirits drinker, while the 'after' pictures have a definite Hollywood dazzle. A smile that unfortunately leaves the rest of his face in the shade.

'I'd recommend it to anyone,' says Bill.

Donald raises the cup to his mouth and the heat from the coffee makes his whole jaw sting.

3

'Fulgurating.'

'What?'

It is a hard word to say with a mouthful of dental swabs, leaning back under the bright light of Dr Purcell's (Dental Technician) investigative, overhead beam, which gleams like an iodine egg.

Donald wonders what brought that thought to his mind.

'The pain,' he mumbles, 'it's like lightning. Like flashes of lightning. Especially if I eat ice cream—'

'Don't talk,' says Dr Purcell.

'Or drink hot coffee.'

'Then don't drink it.'

He pokes about in Donald's mouth, scraping and scratching at the enamel with a sensation not unlike fingernails traversing a blackboard, or a balloon squeaking. Except it is his teeth. It is intimate discomfort. On their tray the little hooks and mirrors look like instruments of inquisition, like something from *Marathon Man*. The sound is like a creature scratching at the centre of his head, tunnelling through his brain. The little suction hose slurps at the moisture underneath his tongue.

'You have a lot of plaque,' says Dr Purcell, disapprovingly.

After he has finished his examination Dr Purcell orders Donald to rinse and spit, which he does. He likes that part. Then he drinks a thimble cup of water. Purcell nods curtly to his assistant who removes her white smock and returns to her other duties as receptionist in the front office.

'Well, there's certainly a bit of work to be done. Crowns. Root canal. Bonding.'

'How much will all that—'

'Oh I'd have to get my girl to work that out. You're right though, it's not cheap. However I don't think I can fit you in until May,' Purcell says, rinsing his tools and placing them in the autoclave. 'We're very busy.'

'I'm thinking of the Thailand option.'

'I would hardly recommend that.'

Dr Purcell has a significant copse of hair in his ears. He's old-school and, as such, never smiles.

'It's much cheaper,' says Donald.

'That may be so,' says Purcell, not bothering to hide his annoyance, 'but there's no guarantee as to the quality of their work. You let me do it and your teeth will outlive you.'

'I know people who swear by it.'

'What sort of people?'

'Smart, intelligent people.'

'The dentist in me,' says Purcell, 'finds that suggestion highly offensive.'

'What? That other people could have a different opinion.'

The dentist turns on him, irritably. 'Well you tootle off in their footsteps if you want to. I think it's highly irresponsible, traipsing off to a place like that at a time like this—a third world country. You need to get your teeth fixed by a professional—'

'They are professionals.'

'Not by some fly-by-night.'

His eyebrows are raised in anger. There is a poster on the wall of some sumptuous tropical island scenery, but it does not seem to be having the soothing effect it is supposed to.

'Do they guarantee their work?' Purcell goes on. 'Better ask them that. What if they botch things up? You won't be able to flit back there so easily to get any running repairs done.'

'I'm hoping they won't botch things up.'

'How long have I been looking after your teeth?'

'I don't know. A long time.'

'And that counts for nothing I suppose. Well off you go. Don't say I didn't warn you.'

Dr Purcell turns his back on Donald who removes his bib, white as a handkerchief of snow, and clambers out of the awkward chair which has all the bells and whistles hanging off it. There is no handshake. Donald goes out to the front office where the young receptionist, who doubles as the old man's assistant, looks decidedly miserable. She presents him with a bill.

'Do you need to make another appointment?' she asks.

'I don't think so.'

4

There is a range of procedures on the menu. He can choose porcelain veneers, porcelain crowns, bridges, dental bonding, dental implants, laser whitening, something called *invisalign,* gum treatment, root canal treatment 'and so much more!' Dr Krong Themavengsa grins from his website, standing in his pristine surgery, his image surrounded by five star testimonials. There is a picture of him arm in arm with a famous Bollywood movie star. Look at those pearly whites. Donald doesn't watch Bollywood, but Susan sometimes does, when she wants to unwind, or else have a bit of a weep. It makes a change, she says, from Merchant Ivory.

The hotel boasts the *Molar Deluxe* suite and enumerates its own attractions, which Donald finds amusing, such as: *carpet! fire alarms! light bulbs!* and so on. Stairs AND elevators! However, to be fair, the pictures do make the rooms look rather ritzy. Orchids.

Champagne in buckets by the bedside. A view towards some distant hills. Plus it's as cheap as chips. So Donald is starting to come round to the idea. There is a sale on airfares for twenty-four hours only.

5

Which is why six weeks later his ears are popping (and jaw throbbing) as the 747 flight from Melbourne descends through some turbulence and cloud cover to Suvarnabhumi Airport. Donald is looking forward to seeing the Grand Palace, and several of the gorgeous temples that the guide book has recommended, but first things first. When the plane door opens he is assaulted by the heat and humidity. It is a physical force. It bludgeons him as he crosses the tarmac which is positively sticky with the heat. The sun fierce and orange, like a hot berry. Already he can feel his nose peeling. His lungs feel scorched, as after a lethal curry.

'What is your purpose in coming to our country?'

'Business,' Donald clips, being familiar with the international language of winks and nods.

After Customs he collects his bags from the carousel and steps outside the terminal building. There seems to be some sort of street parade going on; megaphones encouraging the crowd to chant noisily. Flags and banners fly. There is some singing. Perhaps it is a festival? Donald understands none of it. He glances at the crowd with mild curiosity, more concerned with finding a taxi. There are plenty of rickshaws. A rickshaw seems a little too colonial so soon after landing; in fact within a short space of time he witnesses an accident where the twin tusks of a passing rickshaw appear to have impaled the wheels of a bicycle. An altercation is taking place. Funny foreign anecdote number one: *rodeo rickshaw gores unlucky cyclist.* He can feel himself getting into the holiday spirit.

The taxi driver seems desperate to get away, throwing Donald's bags into the back seat, and not before time, because a rotten tomato comes flying through the air from the direction of the throng and splatters on the road. Aha, he thinks, *la Tomatina.* What a lark. More tomatoes fly. They are chanting, Donald now notes, in some anger. Not a festival then. The tyres of the taxi squeal and they are away. The sights whizz past. Donald looks around at everything, wanting to take it all in, but the driver is speeding, certainly going too fast to take photos, and Donald does not know the phrase for slow down. All he has is a sheet of paper with the address of the hotel—the Themavengsa Hotel, on Ratchadaphisek Road—which is where the taxi duly, perhaps unceremoniously, drops him.

Donald thinks it peculiar and not altogether reassuring that the dentist he has an appointment to meet tomorrow also owns the hotel and has named it after himself. The implications don't bear thinking about. At a pinch it augurs well. As does the lobby when he steps into the revolving door and enters. The temperature is immediately ten degrees cooler. An ornamental pond with a dwarf palm sits in the middle of the foyer. The statue of a white elephant spouts water from its alabaster trunk. Or is it marble? Water feature sound affects. That's what Purcell ought to invest in, to create the right soothing ambience, not a tacky old poster. All about the lobby he spots statues of elephants, some of them two-headed, after the deity whose name escapes Donald at the moment—Ganesh, that's it. Who is Ganesh again? He must look it up.

Behind the desk it is indeed the land of smiles.

'*Sa-wut dee*,' says the receptionist.

'Hello. Do you speak *Ung-grit?*' Donald asks in his best Thai, the phrase book handy in his pocket.

'Yes. Welcome to the Themavengsa Hotel. We hope your stay is happy one. You are Mr Watkins from Croydon?'

'I am,' says Donald, glad of the English.

'Have you stayed with us before, Mr Watkins?'

'This is my first time in your beautiful country.'

'There is a registration form to be completed, plus I shall need your credit card details in case of breakages.'

'Of course, but I don't intend on breaking anything.'

'Pardon of mine?' says the receptionist, mildly alarmed.

'It's all right, I won't break anything.'

'Ah. Thank you.'

What do they think he is going to break? On the counter is a postcard of the same elephant in the fountain pool. Ah, God of good fortune. Remover of obstacles. He takes one so as to write home to Susan when he has a spare moment. Funny foreign observation number two: *lots of elephants.*

6

From his sixth story window Donald looks down on a section of the city where Ratchadapisek Road, bisects the axis of Rama

Road, running from left to right beneath his feet. Donald lays a complimentary map out on the table so as to get his bearings. On this first morning after a disrupted night's sleep—he has woken twice in the darkness not knowing where he is—he looks out at the brilliant Thai morning. The sun seems higher, more distant, yet already Donald can sense the day warming up beyond the thickened, double glazing of the windows. Any distant hills are masked by the haze. He reads all the information brochures about the features of the room, the hotel, the city. A statue of an elephant sits on the television. He has read that the heat of the bitumen roads burns the feet of the real elephants as they ferry tourists about the city. Not such good fortune for them. On principle he vows not to catch an elephant. The festivities from yesterday still seem to be carrying on. Below him, to the right, a parade of revellers moves slowly along the middle of the road. The pulse of whistles, like summer cicadas, rises on the air. Some of the crowd wave placards he cannot read from this height. He wouldn't have understood them anyway. On the view's vertical axis he watches a second group of people coming down Rama Road. This group distinguishes itself by the predominance of red flags and the red shirts they are wearing. He wonders what the celebration is. From his vantage point Donald sees the two groups converge. As each party approaches the intersection chaos breaks out. High above the melee, Donald's eyes widen in astonishment. The two groups charge at each other, collide and merge, like an estuary of milk and blood. The red shirts blend into the other, the way a burst capillary stains the white of an eye. The placards are used as clubs. Both groups attack each other with whatever they can find. The generalised noise of mayhem comes to him, albeit muted, through the thickened glass. From the left, along Ratchadapisek Road he sees an armoured vehicle rumble towards the imbroglio. He hears sirens. He sees tear gas canisters fly, the smoke drifting along the street. He sees the crowd break up and disperse. They flee in every direction. By the time a group of soldiers appears the crowds have mostly gone, the last stragglers pick themselves up and hobble off. It hasn't taken long, the way they vanish up side streets. It is as if he has observed from a great height two species of ant attack each other on a television documentary, wondering what on earth are they fighting over? He wonders if he turns on the television will he be able to find an explanation for what he has just witnessed with his own eyes, for there has been no mention in the guidebook of a festive celebration.

He comes down later in the elevator which opens onto the lobby. The land of smiles is there to greet him behind the desk, fleeting and slightly embarrassed. One of the doormen is raising some metal screens which have been lowered to protect the windows. The revolving door is locked shut. Outside on the street litter and red rags are strewn along the road.

'I trust you sleep well Mr Watkins,' says the concierge behind the desk, whose name tag announces: Mr Vasan Phu.

'Very well, thank you,' says Donald. 'What on earth has been going on?'

'Oh, nothing to worry about. A little posturing. It is the season.'

'Nothing to worry about? Are you sure?'

'Of course. Are you prepared for some breakfast?'

221

7

Dr Krong Themavengsa peers into Donald's mouth. Despite the fact that he is a youngish, fresh faced man with smooth skin and everything to live for, he is not smiling. His moustache consists of about twelve single black hairs spaced out along his upper lip. It is like a cartoon moustache and Donald finds it hard to take seriously. He has explained to Donald the process that is to take place over three sessions, spread several days apart. He explains that time is needed to build the crowns after the initial filing and custom measuring. Of course he will have temporary caps in the meantime and so should not be inconvenienced. Dr Themavengsa's English is good. What Donald can't understand is why he is so palpably twitchy. He must have performed thousands of these procedures judging by the opulence of the hotel that bears his name. Judging, also, by the present rooms it looks to be a successful enterprise. It is also apparent there are several other dentists working out of the clinic, so Donald is pleased he has landed the head man.

'You realise your lower wisdom teeth are impacted,' says the head man, studying Donald's X-rays.

'I do now,' says Donald.

'They will have to come out or else they will cause problems later. That will require a general anaesthetic which one of my colleagues will administer.'

Donald thinks of Bill Middleton's phrase: *the works.*

'I've had a big breakfast this morning. Shouldn't I fast before an anaesthetic?'

'Quite right. Not today,' says Dr Themavengsa. 'We shall incorporate this procedure into our plan.'

He moves over to the window of the surgery, parts the narrow Venetian blinds an inch, and peers out.

'Today we file the stumps.'

'What about some laughing gas?' Donald asks in jest. Since his misspent university days he has always wanted to try laughing gas.

'Yes, that is possible,' Dr Themavengsa answers in all seriousness. 'The anaesthetic qualities of nitrous oxide are not as reliable, but should suffice for this initial procedure. Some patients require no numbing at all. You have a lot of plaque.'

As the dentist is preparing the cylinder he asks, 'The hotel, Mr Watkins, she is comfortable?'

'Yes. Very.'

'This is good. And the food, it is to your taste?'

'Yes. Very nice.'

'That is also good.'

'There was some sort of disturbance outside on the street this morning.'

'Yes?'

'Some sort of riot.'

There is a pause. Dr Themavengsa adjusts some valves on the tank.

'They are protesting at the Government,' he says at last. 'It is very bad.'

'There were two groups,' says Donald.

'The Redshirts approve of Mrs Yingluck Shinawatra, our Prime Minister. The others do not.'

'I see. And you?'

After a significant pause Dr Themavengsa says, 'I think a change of government would be not so bad.'

'The army was there.'

'Yes. It is unfortunate. But not so unfortunate that we cannot carry on with our daily work. Thailand is the land of smiles.'

'So I have heard.'

'They believe there is an imbalance in the political process.'

'They?'

'Many people. Here. Breathe.'

Dr Themavengsa places the rubber mask over his face and Donald's side of the conversation becomes muffled, like a jet pilot at thirty thousand feet. He breathes. He closes his eyes. He thinks he can smell birthday cake.

He is feeling relaxed and mellow, mouth agape, looking at the sparse hairs on Dr Themavengsa's lip. They are like sutures, or ants standing at attention. Donald's jaw is wide open like a clown in a sideshow alley. Themavengsa scrapes and probes and files, selecting a different instrument for each stage of the operation. Nothing hurts. There is soft music playing. Vivaldi. Donald's mouth is thick with swabs. It is like having a mouthful of moths. Themavengsa scratches his nose and Donald giggles.

After half an hour of this scarifying, the door to the outer office quietly opens.

'Not now, not now,' calls Dr Themavengsa, 'I am busy.'

But it is not the receptionist. The figure moves into view beyond the horizon of the dentist's shoulder, like the moon coming up over a mountain, and Donald recognises the unmistakable uniform of a policeman. He moves slowly into Themavengsa's peripheral vision, whose head snaps around. The policeman appears to be someone of high rank judging by the stars on his epaulets, he looks at Dr Themavengsa giving him a slight nod towards the exit. The dentist quickly lays his instruments aside and hurries out of the surgery, closing the door behind him.

The policeman stands over Donald gazing down at him, his mouth clogged with dental swabs. Donald smiles. Or tries to. The hissing tube is still sucking the saliva from his mouth.

'Mr Watkins, my name is Captain Lomahardthai. Perhaps you can why I am here guess?'

Donald shakes his head.

'No no, do not speak. It must be uncomforting,' says the Captain.

Donald nods slightly.

The Captain presses the pedal of the dentist's chair and it subsides smoothly with an oiled sigh. He perches himself awkwardly on the edge of the chair so that his hip, a bony one, comes into contact with Donald's hip. Donald laughs. The Captain's accent is so funny.

'Something is comical, Mr Watkins?'

Donald shrugs, makes a vague gesture with his hand. They obviously mistake him for someone else. The Captain takes the suction tube from Donald's mouth and lays it aside where it continues to gasp for air.

'I think Mr Watkins,' says Captain Lomahardthai, adjusting his sleeves, 'that you have come to Thailand to buy a child.'

Donald creases his brows; shakes his head once.

'A girl, or perhaps a boy.'

What, thinks Donald, is he talking about? Buy a child? The realisation as to the weight of the policeman's words dawns on Donald making him shake his head vigorously.

'Don't try to talk.' Lomahardthai leans closer. 'I understand the temptation. I myself have been tempted.'

One by one he begins to peel the sodden dental swabs from Donald's mouth and, as he speaks, flicks them onto the floor where they fall with a damp plop. Some of them are pink.

'Indeed Mr Watkins, an easy thing it is for a wealthy Westerner. An Australian you are, I think, yes? Twelve thousand Thai Baht— about four hundred of your dollars. But of course this you already know. This is cheap temptation. Very affordable.'

Plop.

Donald manages to squawk, 'My teeth!'

'Yes, your teeth,' says the Captain. 'A common story is. How does it look, Mr Watkins, a single Western man, travelling in Bangkok. All alone. It is an easy leap to conclude. How do you think for us it feels, when some poor farmer comes to Bangkok to sell his child to a Western man? Simply to feed his family. It is a relationship, as is the one between we two, of unequal dimensions. As a nation how do you think this makes us feel?'

Plop.

He has finished extracting the cotton swabs and screws up his nose in distaste at the cavern of Donald's mouth.

'It makes us feel not so good Mr Watkins.'

At this he taps Donald gently on the side of the face.

'A funny name is Mr Watkins, because I am warning you, here in this chair, to leave alone Thai children.'

He taps harder.

'More Australians die in Thailand than any other Asian nation. Why is that I wonder? Thai people welcome visitors to Thailand. We love visitors. But not visitors for Thai children. We want you to visit, spend, enjoy, ride an elephant, but when you leave we want you your sperm to take with you.'

With that he gives a solid slap to Donald's face. A jolt of pain shoots through his jaw—like lightning—and he arches back in the chair. Captain Lomahardthai stares at him a while longer. Then he rises and strolls to the door, from which he turns and raises a finger in naughty admonition. 'When you leave your sperm take with you.'

Donald tastes the blood in his mouth.

8

All flights out of Bangkok have been cancelled, even though the protest leader, Suthep Thaugsuban, has promised the opposition would not blockade the airport. Operation shutdown is in full swing. Donald is stuck. He has only a rudimentary understanding of the politics of the situation. After several frantic phone calls he realises he isn't going anywhere. In the meantime the Australian embassy advises travellers to keep a low profile. After a great deal of anxiety he comes to a conclusion. He may as well wait out the two week hiatus and finish the job. Get his money's worth, however, that policeman, Lomahardthai, has given him a fright. His insinuations are awful. Who have they mistaken him for? He wonders if he can complain to the embassy. Luckily Themavengsa returned after the policeman had gone and put right the damage, which was nervous rather than physical. Rinse and spit, rinse and spit. The dentist seems rather to suggest that the policeman was after a bribe. Donald hadn't thought of that. A bribe. That makes sense. That seems much more straightforward and manageable.

He now has to wait for his next appointment—more molar filing—then a further seven days—(All right, they can squeeze it into six)—while the crowns are made before being fixed to their bases. Then the final surgery: the wisdom teeth. Themavengsa apologises for the political unrest in the country. Very bad timing. People are trying to carry on as normal, but with the army and the police backing the Government it isn't easy. The violence is getting worse. Seven people have been wounded when two motorcycle gunmen open fire on anti-government protesters. In another fracas a policeman has been killed.

My God, thinks Donald, what have I got myself into? Keep a low profile indeed.

From his window two days after his 'interview' with Lomahardthai, he watches smoke rise from a distant part of the city. The day before he had spent all day in bed, shaken, in pain, drinking lime water. Today he is hungry. He catches the elevator down to the lobby. Not wanting to waste his time in urban Bangkok Donald asks the concierge, the man named Phu, if he might visit the famed Golden Temple. No, says Mr Phu, that would be ill-advised. It is too dangerous. Well could Mr Phu recommend a restaurant where Donald might get some lunch? No. Oh, why not? Because the delivery drivers are on strike and there is no one to collect food from the farms. It will all be repaired by tomorrow. But Donald is hungry today. Well, says Mr Phu, there is a popular market two blocks to the south of the hotel where he might find a street stall to serve him with some *kao nee-o,* which Mr Donald might know as sticky rice.

Donald looks left and right as he steps through the door. It is relatively quiet out on the street. Just some innocuous pedestrians. An old woman, without teeth, trying to sell him trinkets. It is still hot. With every step Donald feels he is being followed. He finds the market two blocks away and sees that Themavengsa is right. People are trying to carry on as normal. He orders some *kao nee-o* and feels pleased with himself for attempting the language. He eats in small mouthfuls, the same way he tests the words.

In the street a motor scooter backfires and Donald sees that all about him the people are jumpy, their eyes darting. He sees an elephant, swaying from foot to foot, standing in the sparse shade of a palm tree. He enjoys the market with its strange vegetables and spice-filled, aromatic air. He spots a trestle table laden with nothing but bananas. At last something familiar. He tries to buy one—*neung*—but the banana vendor laughs at him, persuading Donald to buy a hand of ten. They cost next to nothing. After an hour or so he begins to wonder again if he might be being watched, so he returns to the hotel. The old woman, without teeth, is still sitting there. He doesn't want any of her trinkets, but instead gives her a banana. She says something sharpish, and throws the banana at him. He scurries inside and, in a metaphoric sense, barricades himself behind closed doors.

9

A knock at the door wakes him. *Tap tap tap.* It seems to be coming from within the room, not outside. Through the window the lights of the city buildings appear to have been extinguished. He eases himself from the bed. Even the stars have been turned off. Carpet fibres prickle his feet. He is so glad they have carpet and that they had advertised it on their website. There is another knock, louder. The security chain is in place.

'Who is it?'

'Room service.'

What time is it? He opens the door. In the corridor stands Captain Lomahardthai, and beside him a young girl of about nine years of age.

'Your child, Mr Watkins,' says the Captain.

Quickly Donald slams the door. The chain has disappeared. He scurries back to the bed where he pulls up short, seeing himself asleep beneath the sheet, realising he is, himself, still asleep. The city lights are gleaming brightly. The carpet is just carpet. Later he wakes to the sound of fireworks. Only he understands they aren't fireworks.

10

He keeps a low profile. His next appointment with Dr Themavengsa goes uneventfully, although over the following days sporadic gunfire across the city keeps him mostly indoors. Everyone seems to be on tenterhooks. On television the Prime Minister, Mrs Shinawatra appeals for calm as election day approaches. This only seems to inflame the situation. At least Donald assumes she is appealing for calm. He cannot understand the political rhetoric, only the tone of the debate, which seems far from calm and reasoned. He survives on room service. Club sandwiches. And bananas. Occasionally, if Mr Phu tells him it is safe he walks around the immediate block of the hotel, too afraid to venture further. If he sees anyone in a red shirt he turns around and comes back. Delivering his lunch Mr Phu explains that many people feel like this in the current political climate. They feel unsafe. Many people would like to leave for a safer country. Is Australia a safe country? Well, in general, yes. Could Mr Phu bring his wife and family to live in Australia? He is well educated; he would work hard and respect the royal family.

'It's not that simple,' Donald tries to explain.

'Does Australia not like refugees?'

'Well, to put it simply, no.'

'That is a disappointment,' says Mr Phu. 'Australians are such friendly people.'

'I'm sure you would be most welcome, Mr Phu, but perhaps not your whole country.'

'It would not be the whole country.'

'Australians are worried about their jobs.'

'Here, not so much. People are more worried about their lives. Many people have nowhere else to flee to. They must die on the streets.'

'I'm sure it's not as bad as that,' says Donald, but he isn't so sure.

Time slips by. The hotel is its own microclimate.

One day he comes downstairs to find no one at all in the lobby. No Mr Phu, no desk clerk. The screens have been drawn down over the windows again so the light in the foyer is dim. The water feature has been switched off. In the fountain Ganesh is silent.

'Hello,' he calls.

No one answers. He rings the bell. Nothing. He steps behind the desk. The key repository of electronic door cards is full, except for one card, his own. It's here in his pocket. Is this another dream? There is no one in the Manager's office either, where he finds the safe open, devoid of valuables. He picks up the phone, but it is dead. He realises that he is perhaps the only person in the hotel. He can, if he wants, take any key and have his run of the place. However, one antiseptic hotel room, despite all the elephants, would presumably be much the same as any other. Nevertheless, he takes this opportunity to wander the corridors. On the second floor all the guest room doors are open and the beds stripped. A trolley laden with soaps and tiny bottles of shampoo and whisky sits abandoned in the hallway. There is not even a security guard to watch over things. A looter would have a field day, but there are no looters. There is no one. He does not want to break any rules merely for the sake of breaking them. He is a law abiding citizen. Anarchy is not a temptation for him.

He finds his way through some dimly lit corridors to the kitchen. Empty. All the pots and woks hang quietly on their hooks. He opens a fridge, but does not recognise any of the food. Luckily he still has a few bananas left. Donald takes a bottle of juice (mango) and retreats to his room. He gleans from the television coverage that the protesters are occupying Government buildings.

He watches from on high the latest demonstration march down Ratchadaphisek Road. This time there are no Redshirts to meet them, but further down, past Sukhumvit Road, an army vehicle with a water cannon and a platoon of soldiers, or police, or both, wait for them behind their black shields, their batons at the ready. No, anarchy is not a temptation. It's a young person's game. The noise of rioting lasts all day and into the night.

11

The next day the staff have returned and the barricades lifted from the windows. No explanation as to where they have been. The lobby staff are too distracted to ask how he has slept. He's becoming part of the furniture. Donald leaves the hotel early before the city wakes for his last appointment with Dr Themavengsa. He knows by now there are whole ghettos living beneath the freeway overpasses, so he keeps clear of them, not knowing what colour shirt they prefer. He ignores his last bananas sitting on the sideboard, for he knows he must fast before surgery, even though he hasn't been told to. Bit slack on that sort of housekeeping, he thinks. Walking down Ratchadapisek Road he pats his pockets, realises he has left his passport behind. Never mind. It's safe back in his room. Won't need it today. He skulks in doorways waiting for the clinic to open. At one point a military vehicle rumbles up the street but it pays him no heed.

Dr Themavengsa is visibly on edge.

'The political situation,' he explains, 'is very bad today.'

Donald feels wary about letting such a jittery man dig around in his mouth. However, once he settles to his task, once his ordinary routines kick in he calms down. He washes his hands with antiseptic solution before pulling on a pair of rubber gloves. His nerves are steady. He even whistles. He has shaved. One of his colleagues comes in to prepare the syringe. Donald looks away as the needle pricks the back of his hand and the cannula is inserted.

'Count backwards from one hundred please.'

Quickly, with no pain, a great midnight darkness settles over him which not even the light of the brightest star could penetrate.

12

Slowly he wakes as if rising from the depths of a blackened well, moss creeping up the vertical stone, the water lapping at the corners of his lips, the circle of faint light high above him, out of reach ... *tap tap tap* ... until at last he surfaces and opens his eyes. He does not comprehend what he sees, so drifts back ... fades back ... falls back to ...

Tap tap tap.

Time slips by ... and he ... wakes slowly ... Where is he? He rises again up the throat of the well, floating through moss. His eyes scrape open. The ceiling fan turns lazily, one of its ratchet cogs going *click click click* as it revolves, not *tap tap tap*. Not the dog's tail at all.

His mouth is full of moths. Not moss. Gradually his senses return. The room comes into focus. He realises that he is still reclining in the dentist's chair, not the recovery room, the fan is clicking, and also, it dawns on him, that he is covered in blood.

From his chin to his groin, he is soaked. He sits bolt upright, his head swirling with vertigo. A sudden clang, as of a hammer on his skull. His tongue is dry. The tube still at work in his mouth. He yanks it out. He kneads his chest, but it feels whole. Uninjured. He pulls the cotton swabs from his mouth. Plop plop plop. Some of them are dry and stuck to his gums. His tongue probes tentatively the empty corners of his mouth. His wisdom teeth are gone. It is not the mouth his tongue remembers. The landscape has changed. The hard wires of sutures poke from his gums. His cheeks feel swollen.

Cautiously, dizzy with torpor and confusion, he swings his legs to the side of the chair and stands up. Swaying. He grips the chair for balance. There is a puddle of blood on the floor beneath the chair. Only after some murky thought processes does he come to understand that it is not his blood. What a relief. A cannula still protrudes from the back of his hand like a glass splinter. He pulls it out and a dollop of new blood wells there. It is a pain that feels real and holds him in the moment. He welcomes it. On the little tray beside the chair sits a small pile of dental swabs. He grabs one and presses it to his hand until the bleeding stops. But all this other blood? An orgiastic fly drones heavily in the room.

Terribly thirsty, barely able to walk, he makes it to the door. His feet leave crimson prints behind him. Beyond the door the outer office has been trashed. The computer tipped off the desk, the desk overturned, the filing cabinets knocked over, even the floral prints are askew on the walls. There is no receptionist and no dentist. A water cooler in the corner has survived the assault, so Donald rinses his mouth, splashes his face with a handful of water trying to wake himself up. Rinse and spit. There is nowhere to spit so he spits into a pot plant. It doesn't seem to matter much. Slowly the world comes back to him. He finds the change room and manages to slip his trousers on underneath the surgical gown. Why he had to take his trousers off in the first place he doesn't understand. His wallet is still there. The money in it, untouched. Where is his passport? Oh yes, he remembers. His shoes. In a post-anaesthetised daze he leaves the office. His feet leaden and sticky. All he wants is to sleep, to fall, to drift, let this dream be over, but he knows he has to get back to the hotel. He doesn't know what has happened; he only knows he needs to be near his passport. He has no idea what day it is, or how long he's been unconscious.

Utterly drained he makes it down to the street where the last stragglers of the latest demonstration dawdle after the main column. Their collective roar of outrage precedes him down the road by a kilometre or so. Again the street is littered with stones, torn placards, rubbish. An injured man is being helped to his feet by two companions. Donald untangles the bloodied dentist's bib from around his neck. There is still plenty of coagulating blood underneath. Strangely, not many people in the slowly moving crowd give him a second glance. He is blending in. He is not sure if he is following in the footsteps of the opposition protesters, or the Government supporters. He moves as part of a tide. Plodding. He now comprehends the meaning of plodding. His feet feel heavy as stone. Not ordinary stone, but plodding stone.

After a few interminable blocks Donald recognises the produce markets where he bought his bananas. How long ago was that? The familiar sight gives him some heart for, still stunned and baffled, he understands he has to get off the street. Mr Phu will help him if only he can get back to the hotel. One foot at a time. One foot after the other. It is the most exhausting walk he has ever taken.

As he staggers through the market a number of the stall holders stare at him. Suddenly gunfire opens up (no, not fireworks) and there is only a momentary confusion before panic erupts. People scream. Everyone ducks for cover under whatever shelter they can find. A man falls in the road and screams. Thinking quickly several stall holders overturn their trestle tables and people dive for cover behind them. Donald sees fruit and vegetables and fabrics spill onto the ground before he realises that he, too, probably should find cover. All this chaos is like a movie. A dream.

In slow motion he dives behind one of the tables as bullets buzz and ricochet overhead. A part of him wonders, since he is resting here, if he might take a little nap. Forty winks to sleep off the anaesthetic and gather his strength. His heart pounds. The stitches in his gums prod at his cheeks. He realises he is terribly hungry, which must be from the fasting. There is a perfectly good banana just there on the ground. May as well eat it. The adrenaline and anaesthetic fight in his system. Melons burst and, as he watches, people fall in the street. There is pandemonium. Men and women scramble for shelter. To his surprise Donald's old friend the banana seller stands up behind his table, pulls a revolver from beneath his shirt and lets off six quick shots before ducking down again. He seems to be aiming at the upper windows of a nearby building. He grins at Donald.

'Are you hit?' he seems to say.

'No, not at all,' Donald seems to reply, giving a thumbs up.

All around them people are shouting, screaming, crying. Several are writhing on the ground. A few are not moving.

Nearby a child of about eight cries out, '*Mair.*'

Where has she come from? She is staring aghast at a woman who lies across the way behind a low stone wall. An open space of road between them. The child crawls over the people cowering behind the table. She is about to race into the road when Donald sees a bunch of bananas twitch and burst into pulp. Who would shoot bananas? They didn't hurt anyone.

He sees what is about to happen. He grabs the child by the leg and hauls her back behind the table. A bullet blows chips off it.

'*Mair.*'

The woman looks aghast across the empty space between her and her daughter. The banana vendor returns fire, but does he know what window he should be aiming at? Probably not.

Donald grips the terrified child. She tries to bite his hand. He squeezes her into submission. Across the road the mother looks as if she is about to make a dash for it across the gap. Donald holds up his palm to halt her—the universal sign of STOP—and luckily she understands. More bullets pepper the market, pecking like poultry at the ground. More people screaming. With the child in his arms his own fear is partially alleviated. He cannot let her go. He is her protector. The mother stares at them. For twenty minutes they are pinned down like that, some of the stall keepers shooting back until they run out of ammunition. Gunfire echoes across the city. The little girl struggles in Donald's arms.

Then in shock and catatonic resignation she stops struggling and lies motionless. She stares at her mother and her mother stares at her across the no man's land of the road. After a further burst of gunfire she buries her face in his bloodied side, the shirt now crusting and stiff, her fingers in her ears.

Poor Themavengsa, it must have been his blood beneath the chair. The firing becomes sporadic and eventually ceases, but it is impossible to say if they have heard the last shots. It might be a trick. They have to wait.

After twenty more minutes it becomes apparent that the battle has dwindled. They have withdrawn. People moan and sob behind the market barricades. Sirens shriek in the distance. The girl whimpers in Donald's arms. Her mother, head down, races across the road and they are reunited behind the trestle table, their faces very close together. Someone, testing the air like a rabbit, scampers out and drapes a blanket over a body on the road. Someone else stands a table up. These bananas are still in reasonable condition. Back they go on display. It takes a moment for the girl to untangle herself from Donald's coagulated grip, but eventually she does and her mother takes her. They cling to each other, as the wailing rises around them.

13

It takes the lobby staff some time to open the shutters and let him back in. The trinket seller has gone. He stands there banging on the grille. They lock the barricade behind him. When they see the state he's in they want to know if they should call the ambulance. Donald insists in the negative. Outside the hotel it looks like a cyclone has hit the main thoroughfare, though inside Ganesh the elephant spouts water in the fountain. Unfortunately the elevators have stopped working. Luckily there are stairs. Donald wonders if he can crawl up them? Mr Phu helps him to the sixth floor, one step at a time. They have to pause and rest on each landing.

'Come on Mr Watkins, you can do it. Just four more flights.'

They make it. Donald gives him all his remaining Thai currency. He has never felt more exhausted. The hotel room is a place of haven. His passport is right where he left it in the room-safe. As if in a dream he showers (no hot water, but he doesn't care) and collapses on the bed where he sleeps for fourteen hours. He never sees Mr Phu again.

When he finally awakes there is someone in his room. It is one of the receptionists (no smiles now) and with her she has a man Donald has never seen before.

'Do you need to go to the hospital?'

'No,' says Donald. 'Why?'

'The condition you returned in,' says the stranger. 'The staff have been worried.'

'No, I'm fine. It's just that I'm so desperately tired.'

'I am from the embassy,' he says. 'Perhaps you might like to shower.'

He indicates some lingering blood on Donald's neck. Dried now.

Downstairs he has a car. Donald's whole rescue has been organised while he slept. They want to get all Australian citizens out of Bangkok as soon as possible, and Donald isn't complaining. There is an advisory warning on all non-essential travel to Thailand. If sir would care to dress and pack quickly.

Downstairs people slap at the windscreen, clamouring to get in with them, to take them away, anywhere, just away from the conflict. Donald thinks it is hard to tell what they want. Equality? They're prepared to die for that? He feels for them, he really does, as the car moves through the throng with doors locked but, after all he has been through, can't they cut him a little slack?

14

'It sounds like you saved the poor girl's life,' says Susan, after Donald has at last made it home. 'Preventing her from running on the road like that.'

'It felt like I was tormenting her,' he says.

'How?'

'All she wanted was to get to her mother. And I held her back. The way she bit and scratched. I held her back with all my strength.'

'And that's a good thing Don,' says Susan. 'You did a good thing. People don't think clearly in those sorts of situations.'

'I certainly wasn't thinking clearly. I don't think I'm thinking clearly now.'

Donald isn't sure of anything. Nathan is there. He sits on his father's knee listening to the story, glad beyond speaking to have Donald home, safe, alive. Even so, nothing—nothing is a given. He might have been shot. He might have been locked up. The wiry stitches still cut into Donald's tongue. He will have to go and see Purcell to get them out, face that sarcasm.

They sit there, the three of them, the dog too, not speaking in the warmth of the kitchen, a pot bubbling aromatically on the stove, and for a moment none of them move, for a moment the world, its cruelty and craziness, pauses in its incessant tapping.

Acknowledgements

Some of these stories have been previously published, some in slightly different forms. My thanks go to the editors of these journals.

The Eagle, published in *Southerly*, vol. 75, no. 3, 2016

A Handful of Water, published in *Regime* # 3, 2014

White to the End of the World, published in *Antipodes*, vol. 29, no. 2, 2015 (USA)

The Milkman's Son, published in *Heat* # 19, 2009

Morris Minors, published in *Narrator Magazine* # 2, 2012

My Father's Shopping List, published in *Verity La*, 2018

Bluey and Myrtle, published in *The Great Unknown*, ed. Angela Meyer, Spineless Wonders, 2013

Leaving the Diggings, published in *Prosopisia*, vol. viii, no. 1, 2015 (India)

Political Correctness, published in *Southerly,* vol. 70, no. 2, 2010

Boy, Girl, View, published in *Outburst* # 11, 2012 (Ireland)

The Republic of North-Eastern Victoria, published in *Meanjin* vol. 68, no. 2, 2009

Turning the Other Cheek, published in *Westerly* vol. 59.1, 2014

Tooth for a Tooth, published in *Turbine* # 13, 2014 (New Zealand)

A Day in Court, published in *The Moth* # 16, 2014 (Ireland)

Dictation, published in *Four W* # 23, 2012

The Buddy Cell, published in *Four W* # 27, 2016

Young Men and the Sea, published in *Southerly* vol. 63, no. 2, 2003

The Phone Rings, published in *Famous Reporter* # 43, 2011

Reading with Daddy, published in *Antipodes* vol. 28, no. 2, 2014 (USA)

Some of these stories were written with the assistance of a grant from the Literature Board of the Australia Council for the Arts. Their support is greatly appreciated. I would like to thank the University of NSW for the financial support offered by the Alissa McPherson Fellowship. I am also indebted to the Bundanon Trust for a residency at the Arthur Boyd Centre, Bundanon, where some of the later writing took place. Similarly I owe thanks to the Neilma Sidney Literary Travel Fund for support in the mid stages of organising this book. Lastly, but far from least, I would like to thank Andy Kissane, poet, writer and editor extraordinaire, and David Musgrave at Puncher and Wattmann for their energy and commitment to publishing short fiction in Australia. Many thanks.

Born in Melbourne, Mark O'Flynn now lives in the Blue Mountains. His poetry collections include *The Too Bright Sun* (1996), *The Good Oil* (2000), *What Can Be Proven* (2007), *Untested Cures* (2011), *The Soup's Song* (2015), and *Shared Breath* (2017). His short stories and reviews have appeared in a wide range of journals and magazines, both in Australia and overseas. A second novel, *Grassdogs*, one of the winners of the Varuna Manuscript Award, was published in 2006 by Harper Collins, followed by *The Forgotten World*, (2013). A collection of short stories, *White Light*, was also published later that year. He has also published a memoir, *False Start*, (2013). His recent novel, *The Last Days of Ava Langdon*, (UQP, 2016) was shortlisted for both the Miles Franklin Award and the Prime Minister's Literary Award for Fiction, as well as winning the Voss Literary Award, 2017. In 2018 he was a Visiting Fellow at the University of NSW.